# *Praise for* **The Underneath**

• NEWBERY HONOR BOOK •
• NATIONAL BOOK AWARD FINALIST •
• AMAZON.COM'S #1 BOOK OF THE YEAR •
• 2009 PEN USA LITERARY AWARD WINNER FOR CHILDREN'S LITERATURE •
• *NEW YORK TIMES* BESTSELLER •
• ALA NOTABLE BOOK •

★"Joining Natalie Babbitt's *Tuck Everlasting* as a rare example
of youth fantasy with strong American underpinnings."
—*Booklist*, starred review

"*The Underneath* is as enchanting as a hummingbird,
as magical as the clouds."
—Cynthia Kadohata, Newbery Medal–winning author of *Kira-Kira*

"A magical tale of betrayal, revenge, love and the importance
of keeping promises."—*Kirkus Reviews*

"A mysterious and magical story; poetic yet loaded with suspense."
—Louis Sachar, Newbery Medal–winning author of *Holes*

"[A] fine book . . . most of all distinguished by the originality of
the story and the fresh beauty of its author's voice—a natural
for reading aloud."—*Horn Book Magazine*

"Rarely do I come across a book that makes me catch my breath, that
reminds me of why I wanted to be a writer. . . . A classic."
—Alison McGhee, author of the *New York Times* bestselling *Someday*

"An extraordinary tale of epic scope."
—*Los Angeles Times*

"Kathi Appelt's novel, *The Underneath*, reads like a ballad sung."
—Ashley Bryan, Hans Christian Andersen Award nominee and
three-time Coretta Scott King Award medalist

"[Exerts] an almost magnetic pull that draws the reader into the book's
trackless, treacherous world."
—*The Wall Street Journal Online*

"Every so often a literary work of surpassing beauty arrives in
the unlikely guise of a book for children or young teens. There is a deep
and inexplicable magic underlying the apparent simplicity of such works.
From the gemlike *Goodnight Moon* to novels such as *The Wind in the Willows*
or *A Wrinkle in Time*, children's literature is that place where a young, open
mind can catch life-changing glimpses of the majesty of the written word.
Twin narratives, spinning like twin tornadoes, on course to merge into
a perfect storm—and, if this critic can hazard such a prediction,
into a modern classic."
—*San Antonio Express–News*

"Haunting in tone and resonance, *The Underneath* weaves
a heartrending and magical tale that speaks to love and hope, loneliness
and loss, ancestral forgiveness and a deep abiding reverence for the natural
world that surrounds us, the ethereal world that entices our imagination and
the real world that may bruise us, haunt us, but eventually set us free."
—The National Book Foundation

"Appelt in her debut novel has somehow managed to write a book
that I've been describing to people as (and this is true) *Watership Down*
meets *The Incredible Journey* meets *Holes* meets *The Mouse and His Child*."
—Elizabeth Bird/Fuse #8

# The
# Underneath

# The
# Underneath

by **Kathi Appelt**

WITH DRAWINGS BY DAVID SMALL

Atheneum Books for Young Readers

new york london toronto sydney

*For Greg and Cynthia, because there is love*
*and then there are cats,*
*and aren't the two the same*
*—K. A.*

ATHENEUM BOOKS FOR YOUNG READERS
An imprint of Simon & Schuster Children's Publishing Division
1230 Avenue of the Americas, New York, New York 10020
This book is a work of fiction. Any references to historical events, real people,
or real locales are used fictitiously. Other names, characters, places, and incidents are
products of the author's imagination, and any resemblance to actual events
or locales or persons, living or dead, is entirely coincidental.
Text copyright © 2008 by Kathi Appelt
Illustrations copyright © 2008 by David Small
All rights reserved, including the right of reproduction in whole or in part in any form.
ATHENEUM BOOKS FOR YOUNG READERS is a registered trademark of Simon & Schuster, Inc.
For information about special discounts for bulk purchases, please contact
Simon & Schuster Special Sales at 1-866-506-1949 or business@simonandschuster.com.
The Simon & Schuster Speakers Bureau can bring authors to your live event. For more
information or to book an event, contact the Simon & Schuster Speakers Bureau
at 1-866-248-3049 or visit our website at www.simonspeakers.com.
Also available in an Atheneum Books for Young Readers hardcover edition.
Book design by Russell Gordon
The text for this book is set in Bembo.
The illustrations for this book are rendered in Prismacolor pencil.
Manufactured in the United States of America
1210 FFG
First Atheneum Books for Young Readers paperback edition January 2010
6  8  10  9  7  5
The Library of Congress has cataloged the hardcover edition as follows:
Appelt, Kathi, 1954–
The underneath/Kathi Appelt ; illustrated by David Small.
p.        cm.
Summary: An old hound that has been chained up at his hateful owner's run-down shack,
and two kittens born underneath the house, endure separation, danger, and many other tribulations.
ISBN 978-1-4169-5058-5 (hc)
[1. Survival—Fiction. 2. Dogs—Fiction. 3. Cats—Fiction. 4. Bayous—Fiction.]
I. Small, David, 1945– ill. II. Title.
PZ7.A6455Un 2008
[Fic]—dc22
2007031969
ISBN 978-1-4169-5059-2 (pbk)

THERE IS NOTHING lonelier than a cat who has been loved, at least for a while, and then abandoned on the side of the road. A small calico cat. Her family, the one she lived with, has left her in this old and forgotten forest, this forest where the rain is soaking into her soft fur.

How long has she been walking? Hours? Days? She wasn't even sure how she got here, so far from the town where she grew up. Something about a car, something about a long drive. And now here she is. Here in this old forest where the rain slipped between the branches and settled into her fur. The pine needles were soft beneath her feet; she heard the water splash onto the puddles all around, noticed the evening roll in, the sky grow darker.

She walked and walked, farther and farther from the red dirt road. She should have been afraid. She should have been concerned about the lightning, slicing the drops of rain in two and electrifying the air. She should have been worried in the falling dark. But mostly she was lonely.

She walked some more on the soft pine needles until at last she found an old nest, maybe a squirrel's, maybe a skunk's, maybe a porcupine's; it's hard to tell when a nest has gone unused for a long time, and this one surely had. She was grateful to find it, an old nest, empty, a little dry, not very, but somewhat out of the rain, away from the slashes of lightning, here at the base of a gnarled tupelo tree, somewhere in the heart of the piney woods. Here, she curled up in a tight ball and waited, purred to her unborn babies. And the trees, the tall and kindly trees, watched over her while she slept, slept the whole night through.

AHH, THE TREES. On the other side of the forest, there is an old loblolly pine. Once, it was the tallest tree in the forest, a hundred feet up it reached, right up to the clouds, right beneath the stars. Such a tree. Now broken in half, it stands beside the creek called the Little Sorrowful.

Trees are the keepers of stories. If you could understand the languages of oak and elm and tallow, they might tell you about another storm, an earlier one, twenty five years ago to be exact, a storm that barreled across the sky, filling up the streams and bayous, how it dipped and charged, rushed through the boughs. Its black clouds were enormous, thick and heavy with the water it had scooped up from the Gulf of Mexico due south of here, swirling its way north, where it sucked up more moisture from the Sabine River to the east, the river that divides Texas and Louisiana.

This tree, a thousand years old, huge and wide, straight and true, would say how it lifted its branches and welcomed the heavy rain, how it shivered as the cool water ran down its trunk and washed the dust from its long needles. How it sighed in that coolness.

But then, in that dwindling of rain, that calming of wind, that solid darkness, a rogue bolt of lightning zipped from the clouds and struck. Bark flew in splinters, the trunk sizzled from the top of the crown to the deepest roots; the bolt pierced the very center of the tree.

A tree as old as this has a large and sturdy heart, but it is no match for a billion volts of electricity. The giant tree trembled for a full minute, a shower of sparks and wood fell to the wet forest floor. Then it stood completely still. A smaller tree might have jumped, might have spun and spun and spun until it crashed onto the earth. Not this pine, this loblolly pine, rooted so deep into the clay beside the creek; it simply stood beneath the blue-black sky while steam boiled from the gash sixty feet up, an open wound. This pine did not fall to the earth or slide into the creek. Not then.

And not now. It still stands. Most of its branches have cracked and fallen. The upper stories have long ago tumbled to the forest floor. Some of them have slipped into the creek and drifted downstream, down to the silver Sabine, down to the Gulf of Mexico. Down.

But the trunk remains, tall and hollow, straight and true. Right here on the Little Sorrowful, just a mile or so from a calico cat, curled inside her dry nest, while the rain falls all around.

MEANWHILE, DEEP BENEATH the hard red dirt, held tightly in the grip of the old tree's roots, something has come loose. A large jar buried centuries ago. A jar made from the same clay that lines the bed of the creek, a vessel with clean lines and a smooth surface, whose decoration was etched by an artist of merit. A jar meant for storing berries and crawdads and clean water, not for being buried like this far beneath the ground, held tight in the web of the tree's tangled roots. This jar. With its contents: A creature even older than the forest itself, older than the creek, the last of her kind. This beautiful jar, shaken loose in the random strike of lightning that pierced the tree's heart and seared downward into the tangled roots. Ever since, they have been loosening their grip.

Trapped, the creature has waited. For a thousand years she has slipped in and out of her deep, deep sleep, stirred in her pitch-black prison beneath the dying pine. *Ssssoooonnnn*, she whispered into the deep and solemn dark, *my time will come*. Then she closed her eyes and returned to sleep.

# 4

IT WASN'T THE chirring of the mourning doves that woke the calico cat, or the uncertain sun peeking through the clouds, or even the rustling of a nearby squirrel. No, it was the baying of a nearby hound. She had never heard a song like it, all blue in its shape, blue and tender, slipping through the branches, gliding on the morning air. She felt the ache of it. Here was a song that sounded exactly the way she felt.

*Oh, I woke up on this bayou,*
*Got a chain around my heart.*
*Yes, I'm sitting on this bayou,*
*Got a chain tied 'round my heart.*
*Can't you see I'm dyin'?*
*Can't you see I'm cryin'?*
*Can't you throw an old dog a bone?*
*Oh, I woke up, it was rainin',*
*But it was tears came fallin' down.*
*Yes, I woke up, it was rainin',*
*But it was tears came fallin' down.*
*Can't you see I'm tryin'?*

*Can't you hear my cryin'?*
*Can't you see I'm all alone?*
*Can't you throw this old dog a bone?*

She cocked her ears to see which direction it came from. Then she stood up and followed its bluesy notes, deeper and deeper into the piney woods. Away from the road, from the old, abandoned nest, away from the people who had left her here with her belly full of kittens. She followed that song.

FOR CATS, A hound is a natural enemy. This is the order of things. Yet how could the calico cat be afraid of a hound who sang, whose notes filled the air with so much longing? But when she got to the place where the hound sang, she knew that something was wrong.

She stopped.

In front of her sat a shabby frame house with peeling paint, a house that slumped on one side as if it were sinking into the red dirt. The windows were cracked and grimy. There was a rusted pickup truck parked next to it, a dark puddle of thick oil pooled beneath its undercarriage. She sniffed the air. It was wrong, this place. The air was heavy with the scent of old bones, of fish and dried skins, skins that hung from the porch like a ragged curtain.

Wrong was everywhere.

She should turn around, she should go away, she should not look back. She swallowed. Perhaps she had taken the wrong path? What path should she take? All the paths were the same. She felt her kittens stir. It surely wouldn't be safe to stay here in this shabby place.

She was about to turn around, when there it was again—the song, those silver notes, the ones that settled just beneath her skin. Her kittens stirred again, as if they, too, could hear the beckoning song. She stepped closer to the unkempt house, stepped into the overgrown yard. She cocked her ears and let the notes lead her, pull her around the corner. There they were, those bluesy notes.

*Oh, I woke up, it was rainin',*
*But it was tears came fallin' down.*
*Yes, I woke up, it was rainin',*
*But it was tears came fallin' down.*
*Can't you see I'm tryin'?*
*Can't you hear my cryin'?*
*Can't you see I'm all alone?*
*Can't you throw this old dog a bone?*

Then she realized, this song wasn't calling for a bone, it was calling for something else, someone else. Another step, another corner. And there he was, chained to the corner of the back porch. His eyes were closed, his head held back, baying.

She should be afraid, she should turn around and run, she should climb the nearest tree. She did not. Instead, she simply walked right up to this baying hound and rubbed against his front legs. She knew the answer to his song, for if she could bay, her song would be the same.

Here.

Right here.

Ranger.

# 6

LIGHTNING IS NOT the only thing that strikes. On the very same night twenty-five years ago when that single blinding bolt struck the old loblolly pine beside the creek, there was a boy. A boy who prowled the mean streets of south Houston in the run-down neighborhoods next to the Ship Channel.

A boy who embraced the darkness, darkness filled with huge, gray wharf rats that scurried along the rafters beneath the tar-coated piers of the docks—scavengers; once he caught one in a crab trap and kept it there, hidden, watched it slowly die from hunger and thirst. Watched it while it twisted against the wooden slats of the trap, desperate in its hunger, fierce in its desperation.

Here was this boy whose father worked on the wharves, his shoulders broad and thick from loading and unloading the ships all day, who spent his free evenings at the Deep Channel Bar, a place that served only dockworkers and the women who served them, a man who drank the hard-edged vodka brought in from Russia and the bitter gin from England, who stumbled home, just as hard-edged and bitter as the vodka and gin.

This boy, a boy who sneered at kindness, even from his mother, his mother who loved flowers and birds.

When she finally left him and his hard-edged father, the boy never even missed her, his timid mother with her small garden behind the house, her pitiable birdbath that he had laced with rat poison one evening while she slept. The last time he saw her, she was holding the body of a bright red cardinal in her hands, so red it could have been blood. He laughed. Laughed at the bloodred feathers, dripping between her fingers, at her, his mother with the cardinal in her palms.

Beware this cruel boy, this boy of darkness.

This boy who had a name once, a real name, whose father, in a drunken rage, caught the boy's face with the side of his fist and broke the bones in his left cheek, split the skin of that tender boy cheek and left a deep and ugly gash. The boy gasped in a blaze of pain. And the father hit him again, then fell to the floor, passed out at last.

Any other boy might have felt sorry for himself; he might have stood over his hideous father and wept. But not this boy. This boy stood in the shabby house where he grew up, took one look around, and glowered. Hatred, like sweat, coated his skin. Blood oozed from the corner of his mouth.

He picked up his father's brand-new rifle and walked into the dark, damp streets of south Houston, his nose dripping, his right eye swollen shut, his jaw never able to close properly again. He walked. Past the docks, the ships with their flags from India and Liberia and Austria, their holds full of spicy curry, of baby monkeys poached from the jungles, of aged red wine in caskets made of ancient oak. Past the concrete warehouses and broken-down houses of the southeast end of Houston. His face burned. He walked. Past all that, past the ships, the refineries, the marshy bayous of the steaming city. Into the deep, dank forest, trees so dense they blocked the sky, kept the hated sun off his shattered face. A boy. On foot for three hundred miles, three hundred miles north of Houston. Disappeared into the woods, hung his real name, whatever it was, on a post oak tree, carved it there and never looked back, never used that name again.

Lightning struck a tree. A father struck his son. A boy struck out.

This boy, whose broken face now resembled the prehistoric fish that still swam in the muddy waters of the bayous, half fish, half alligator. A gar. The most vicious of the scale-and-fin crew. Beware his razor sharp teeth, his steel-trap jaws, his eyes that glow in the murky water.

Here then is a hard-edged bitter boy become a man known as Gar Face. For twenty-five years, while the old loblolly pine shed its branches and bark into the Little Sorrowful Creek and watched them drift toward the sea, Gar Face has roamed this hidden forest. Here, underneath the canopy of the watching willows and birches and ash. Over this past quarter century, the years have softened the old pine. Not so Gar Face. Do not cross his angry path. Do not.

# 7

AT FIRST THE hound was surprised. What was a cat doing here? In his yard? Oh yes, there were cats in the forest, he had seen their shadows at the edge of his vision. But none had ever entered his domain before, wouldn't think of crossing the edge of the twenty-foot circle that was marked by his chain. He had warned them to stay back, just as he had warned the raccoons and the possums and the occasional snake. Stay back. This time, he just stood there while this cat walked right up to him.

He looked down at her, this small calico cat, purring now, and he knew through and through. Here was someone who had found him all alone. Here was someone who walked right up to him and rubbed against his sturdy front legs, stood on her hind legs and licked his silky ears, who touched his brown nose with her small pink one. At long last, after so many years of being tied up in this corner, chained to a post, here was someone who understood his song.

# 8

THIS PINEY WOODS forest in far East Texas is wet and steamy. Take a step and your footprint will fill with water. Look up and you will barely see the sky, only small blue puzzle pieces, blocked by the ancient trees. It is hidden, this place, and so are its denizens.

Watch out for its sluggish bayous and tumbling creeks. There are oxbows and fens that make small lakes here and there. Beware the vipers, the rattlers and corals, the copperheads, the venomous crew. Then there are the non-poisonous varieties, the black snakes, the corn snakes, the rat snakes. Even though they are not toxic, they can still pack a bite.

In these waters there are also snapping turtles, box turtles, sawback turtles, that have lived here for well over a hundred years, old centenarians, and bullfrogs whose songs make the needles on the pines rattle.

Crawdads scoot backward in the gumbo-like water of the bayous.

But the rulers of these swampy glens are the alligators.

They swim just below the surface, the same color as the water, brown-gray, their backs resemble a floating tree.

Nothing scares an alligator, especially the alligators of the Bayou Tartine, the large stream that flows to the west of the Little Sorrowful Creek. It flows through the heart of these forgotten woods. Halfway down the Bayou Tartine, the land drops off in a channel, which creates just enough room for a little bayou, the Petite Tartine. It makes a semicircle and rejoins its big sister, and all the land between is marsh and swamp and quicksand.

Do not go into that land between the Bayou Tartine and its little sister, Petite Tartine. Do not step into that shivery place. Do not let it gobble you up. Stay away from the Tartine sisters.

## 9

GAR FACE, FROM his ratty old pirogue, first saw the beast while he floated down the Bayou Tartine. He trapped and skinned a lot of animals, beavers, foxes, rabbits, even an occasional skunk. But it was alligators that called to him. It was alligators, the soft skin of their bellies, the piercing beams from their yellow eyes, eyes that looked directly at him, alligators. When he looked into the eyes of other animals, all he saw was fear and panic. Not so the gators. They feared no one, not a single soul.

Gar Face cared little for the deer and wild hogs and raccoons that he shot and killed every day. But the gators were a different matter.

Now here he was, just before dawn, just as the light began to weave its way between the limbs of the towering trees, a soggy pre-dawn morning, when the air was so wet it felt as though he needed gills to breathe, when the humidity clung to him like a second skin, that gray morning of unbearable sticky stillness. Gar Face pushed against the pole as he stood in his flat-bottomed pirogue, a kerosene lantern hanging from the bow. Just as he passed the Petite Tartine, he looked over his shoulder and rubbed his eyes.

Had he just seen what he thought he saw? The black rum that he had drunk the night before still lingered behind his eyes. The night had been long, too long.

"Couldn't be," he said out loud. "Only place gators grow that big's in Africa." He looked back over his shoulder, then grabbed the lantern and held it out over the water, but all he saw was a pair of eddies, twin whirlpools swirling on the glassy surface. He shrugged and dipped his pole again. Then shook his head. Only something enormous, sinking fast, could cause whirlpools that far apart. The eddies were at least a hundred feet from one to the other. Was there a beast a hundred feet long, sinking to the bottom of the Bayou Tartine?

Gar Face felt the hair on his arms stand up. The vein in his neck pulsed. The word "respect" floated in the thick and heavy air surrounding him. *Respect* buzzed in his ears, like a thousand hungry mosquitoes. He swatted at his face and neck, but couldn't shoo away the hissing sound the word made on his tongue. *Respect*. He swallowed the word whole and licked his lips.

Only a fool would fail to respect a beast like that. *Respect*. A word he had never had any truck with. *Respect*. It crawled down his back like a rat. He reached around as if to catch it, then held his empty hand in front of his hideous face. *Respect*. He wanted it.

As he poled his boat along, a fine mist began to come down, bringing with it a small amount of coolness. *I'll be back*, he thought. Then he turned toward his tilting house. "Yes, I'll

be back." This time he said it out loud, as if to seal the deal. He shoved the pole into the mud.

We are all of us composed of cells, cells that join together and fuse to make blood and skin and bones, but at the root of all these are needs. Gar Face's needs were simple. He satisfied them with basic things like food and water and shelter and a nightly bottle of something hard-edged and bitter, gin or vodka or rum, rum that eased him through the night and into the early morning. But as he made his way to the tilting house, he could feel the cells in his body gathering up into a tangled mass of yearning, yearning for something stronger than liquor. *Respect.* The yearning dug at him, dug into his very core, formed an ache, like a fist in his solar plexus, hard and unyielding, but it was an ache he liked. He clung to it.

He would get that alligator. The Alligator King. Or he would die trying. He dug his pole into the thick brown water and the rain began to fall.

RANGER. THAT WAS the hound's name. He loved the calico cat straightaway. But he knew he had to alert her to the danger she was in. He pointed out the pelts of foxes and muskrats and mink nailed to the front porch railing, the skins of alligators and rattlesnakes that lay beside them on the slats of the porch. It was Gar Face, he said, the man who kept this old hound chained. Gar Face.

"If he finds you . . . ," Ranger said, and he looked over both shoulders . . . but he couldn't finish. Gar Face was mean. And then there was the rifle that he carried with him always. The Rifle.

Ranger knew about the rifle. Long ago, how many years he couldn't say, he had gone along with Gar Face when he hunted, had run by his side, watched when he aimed the gun and shot the raccoons and the white-tailed deer. And then there was the night, that awful night, when Ranger cornered a bobcat, a beast with glowing eyes. Ranger bayed, bayed his victory song, but just as Gar Face aimed at the cat, had the creature in his crosshairs, Ranger sensed that something was wrong. He moved, and Gar Face shot Ranger instead.

There had been no apologies on the part of the man, just a swift kick in the side from his steel-toed boot, a kick that burned as hot as the bullet lodged in his leg.

"You stupid dog!" the man had snarled.

Then he left Ranger and staggered home, leaving the dog to limp after him, and later chained him to the post, useful only as an alarm, as a hound who bayed when animals came too close, a dog trapped in a twenty-foot circle. That's what Ranger had become, nothing more.

The wound in his leg eventually closed, but the bullet was still lodged there, a daily reminder, yes. But it wasn't the bullet so much as the chain that ate into him, the chain that bound him to the porch post, bound him to the man.

Ranger knew that a small cat would be doomed in the hands of Gar Face. He might use her for target practice with his old rifle, the one he kept strapped across his back. He might use her as alligator bait, tie her to a rope and set her by the water, by the swamp where the alligators floated unseen, just below the

surface of the brown, stagnant water of the Bayou Tartine, alligators who would snap a small cat in half with a single bite. Gar Face might do anything.

"But I have nowhere else to go," said the calico cat. And even though Ranger knew he should make her leave, he also knew that after so many years of being alone, of being chained to the post, he couldn't stand the thought of her going. He shook his head so that his long ears flapped against both sides of his neck.

"Then you must keep out of sight of Gar Face," he said. And together they curled up in the dark space beneath the porch. The Underneath. The dark and holy Underneath.

Whenever there is a breeze in the old forest, you might, for a moment, realize that the trees are singing. There, on the wind, are the voices of sugarberry and juniper and maple, all telling you about this hound, this true-blue hound, tied to a post. They have been watching him all these years, listening to his song, and if he knew what the trees were singing, it might be about how he found a friend.

## II

IT TAKES A long time for a hundred-foot alligator to grow. In this forgotten forest, one year turns into another, until centuries have passed. No one keeps records. No one but the trees. They do not count time in years. If they did, perhaps a thousand might have passed, maybe more, since the day the alligator emerged from his leathery egg, no longer than a man's thumb, smaller than that. He could have become a snack for an egret or an osprey or a bald eagle. He could have been swallowed up by a larger gator. This is what happened to most of his sisters and brothers. But he was swift and cagey from the start. He discovered all the underwater caves, he found the darkest shadows for hiding from the sharp beaks of the large birds, the herons and cranes.

He avoided the other gators, the large ones, the small ones, even his own family. When he was small, he dined on insects, the mosquitoes and dragonflies that landed on the water's surface. Later he found minnows and tadpoles. As the long years passed, he grew and grew, and so did his prey. He became adept at hunting all the water creatures, but he was also nimble on the soft, marshy ground, where he lurked in the mud, camouflaged by his thick and bumpy brownish green skin, the same shades as the water and the boggy land around it. Soon he feasted on marsh rabbits and squirrels, beavers and mink.

His patience was unlimited and his sense of smell was sharp. He knew when an animal was weak or injured, and he waited for it, tracked it down, and struck. Death was swift, for he did not bandy about in torture. He simply grabbed the victim by the throat, snapped its neck, and dragged it to the brown water. There, he spun it, once, twice, three times, and carried it to the bottom of the thick bayou and held it there. Later, the body waterlogged, the Alligator King finished it off.

Afterward he floated just beneath the surface of the water and napped, napped until it was time to dine again.

Any unsuspecting animal could become his dinner: a deer, a peccary, a fox. He was not discerning. Any animal, large or small, made a meal. He was the master of disguise, and he knew how to avoid the quicksand. He had watched many creatures sink out of sight in those shivery sands. But if they made it across the sand or if they somehow got free, he was there, waiting with his sharp teeth and his powerful jaws. Waiting.

Can an alligator live for a thousand years, maybe more? Who's to say? And why not? In this deep, dark forest, this hidden-from-view forest, the gator is not the only ancient being. Certainly, there are trees here that have stood for longer. They are the ones who know the histories of all the species. If a tree can live for a thousand years or more, why not an alligator?

Before the man spotted him, only a few knew that the marshy land between the Bayou Tartine and the Petite Tartine was the secret lair of the Alligator King. Only the other alligators and the trees, and the birds that flew overhead.

And one other.

The one who was trapped in the beautiful jar beneath the tall and dying loblolly pine. The Alligator King blinked his golden eyes and whispered, "Soon, my sister. Your time will come." Then he sank beneath the muddy water.

Alone in her silent cell, Grandmother blinks. Perhaps the Alligator King is a thousand years old, but she, the creature in the jar, is older than that. Much.

# 12

GIVE US A bloodhound, a hound who is bred for the chase, for the hunt, for the full round moon to bay at. That is what Ranger was. A bloodhound. This breed is known for their acute sense of smell. They can hold their noses to the ground and find the toddler who has strayed from his back door, locate the fireman beneath the smoldering crumble of a building, discover the horse that has escaped from its pen.

Yes, the bloodhound is known for his sense of smell. But some, like Ranger, also have a keen sense of hearing. A dog who has been tied to the same place for so many years is familiar with all the sounds around him. He knew the chirring of the cicadas, the peeping of the tree frogs, the creak of the restless pines rooted into the deep red clay. He could identify the throaty growl of a mother raccoon when her cubs wander too far astray, and he knew the invisible whoosh of the great horned owl that slipped across the night sky right at dusk.

He was also acutely aware of the sound of the old pickup as it rumbled away from the yard in the evenings, and again when it moved toward the house the next morning. Once he heard the engine's rumble in the distance, he knew exactly how long it would take for the truck to appear in the yard and how long he had to make sure that the calico was safely tucked beneath the house before Gar Face stepped out of the cab, the door squeaking open and then slamming shut.

He knew the crack of the horrible rifle and the way the bullet split the humid air. These were familiar sounds to Ranger.

But now, there was a new sound in his ears, a soft, low, fluttery sound. Anyone who knows a cat can recognize it—a purr.

Cats are famous for purring. And this is what the calico cat did as she curled up next to Ranger's massive chest, safe and soft. Until he heard it, Ranger had not realized how much he needed this sweet, friendly sound. How much he needed someone to settle in next to him. He didn't know that he needed to not be so solitary until at last he wasn't. So many needs in one old dog.

And while the calico purred into his ears, he realized he had another need—to tell a story. As it turns out, loneliness makes a well for stories, and now that Ranger was no longer alone, his stories began to bubble up. As the calico listened, Ranger told her all about when he was a puppy, when his mother taught him how to put his nose to the ground, how to follow the scent, how to bay at the moon's full face. That was before Gar Face took him.

"But you had those good times to remember," said the cat.

"Yes," he replied with a deep heave of his chest. He did have those good times.

Then she told him of her own good times when she was a kitten with her brothers and sisters, all the games they played, silly games, kitten games. That was before she was taken to the pound, before she was forsaken by her family in town and left on the side of the road. That was before she met Ranger. She licked the hound's silky ears. He loved this. Loved to have his ears washed by this small cat. "I had those good times to remember, too," she added. Then she settled in next to him, close. They had these good times to remember. But the best was yet to come.

Kittens!

They arrived on a moonlit night. The calico cat gave birth as she lay right against Ranger's chest. She listened to his steady heartbeat as one after the other she delivered two beautiful babies. One boy. One girl. She was astonished at their identical sameness, two kittens exactly alike. Silver from head to toe. Silver like the stars that peeked down through the night sky. The same. But then she looked again, looked at the boy cat. On his forehead was a tiny white patch of fur, just above his eyes. A small crescent moon. Yes, her little boy cat bore the moon's own mark. Then she looked at her little girl kitten, small and round, and smiled.

The calico knew that a kitten born in the presence of a hound was rare. *Surely*, she thought, *this will hold them in good stead. This will give them courage.*

Alas, these kittens will need it.

At first they were so tiny, no larger than Ranger's big toes, not quite that large, and all they did was offer up soft, almost imperceptible mewls. For days they stayed tucked beneath their mama, attached to her milky belly. To Ranger they were just mewls and milk, so small he barely noticed them. But kittens grow fast. Mewling and milk were only temporary.

Soon enough, they opened their eyes and began to venture away from the calico cat. At first they wobbled. Then they tottered. And before they were the size of Ranger's nose, they climbed! And what did they climb, or rather who did they climb? Ranger! They dug their tiny little claws into his coppery red fur.

No father has ever been prouder of his brood. Ranger watched over his cat family like the pharaohs watched over the Nile, like the stars watched over the sleeping Earth, like the beach watched over the sea. He never took his eyes off of them, sleeping only when they slept, eating only when they ate. And what he loved most: to hear their purrs. There was nothing finer.

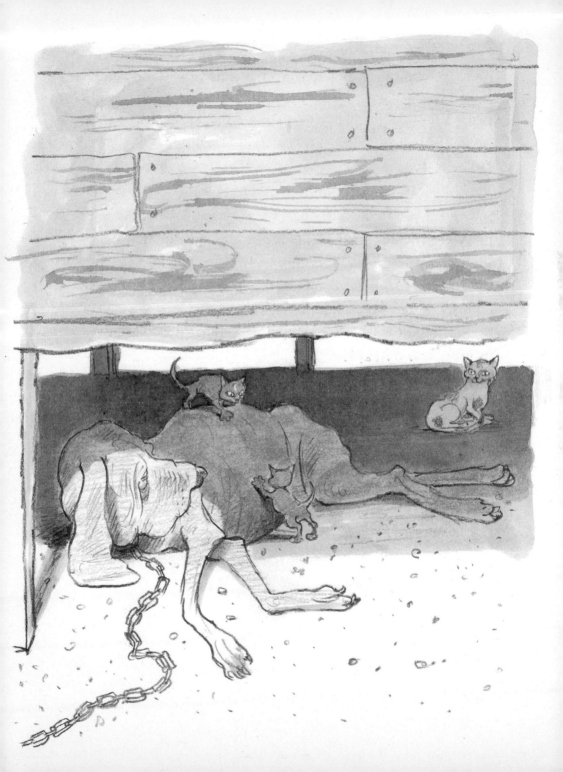

# 13

IN ANOTHER PART of the forest, the old tree that stands by the creek has given up its upper limbs. One by one they've tumbled to the ground, taking the lower ones with them. Bit by bit, the tree is coming down.

And little by little, the jar, the old jar that is trapped beneath its roots, is coming loose. This jar.

Before the ancient potter fired it, she pressed her thumbnail into the soft red clay over and over, a hundred times, a hundred crescent moons that ring its rim. Inside, the creature stirs. Trapped.

And the other trees, the yaupons, the beautyberries, the red oaks shiver beneath the watching stars and glimmery moon.

"Grandmother," they whisper. "Grandmother is waking up."

*Ssssoooooonnnnn*, she says, *my time is coming. Ssssoooonnn!*

# 14

SHE HAS BEEN trapped for a thousand years. But she is older than that, much older. *Lamia*. She is cousin to the mermaids, the ondines, the great sealfolk known as selkies, perhaps the very last of her kind. Clothed in her serpent shape, she swam up the great river to the east, the silver Sabine. She swam in her scaly skin, so black it looked blue. So sleek it gleamed. For ten thousand years she had swam the seven seas, floated on the great Sargasso, sailed along on the mighty currents. And oh, she loved the open oceans.

But once she found the great pine forest, this pine forest, she slipped out of the brackish water and slithered onto the boggy ground. She looked around at the deep and lazy bayous filled with turtles and fish, the giant palmettos, an abundance of rodents, perfect for hunting. She loved the darkness provided by the welcoming trees, the oaks and cedars, the shumards and willow. And the snakes! Here were millions of her reptilian relatives, the small and deadly corals, the bronze-colored copperheads, the massasaugas and their cousin rattlers.

*Ssssssiiiiisssstttterrr,* they said. The air hummed with their voices. She listened again.

*Sssssiiiiiisssssttttterrr!!!* The sound of it settled on her skin. All around, the forest sizzled with the sound of her cousins, large and small and in between. Once more, they called to her.

*Ssssiiisssstttterr!!!*

"Ahh," she replied, "home."

And there she stayed, stayed so long that she became as much a part of the forest as the silent panthers and the black bear, stayed so long that she became known as Grandmother Moccasin. *Sssssss.* Do not look into that mouth of cotton. Do not.

# 15

IN THE DEEP and muddy Bayou Tartine, the Alligator King floated to the surface. Already today he has eaten a dozen turtles. Caught them sleeping in the dappled sun atop a cypress root. He was always hungry. Always. Before the night fell, he would eat a giant bullfrog, a wounded mink, and several fish. Fish are his primary sustenance, the fist-size perch and bottom-dwelling catfish, but he prefers the creatures of the land. They're not quite so salty.

Beware.

# 16

ONE MORNING, RANGER asked the mama cat if they could name the kittens.

"Of course," she said. Ranger knew this was an important task, and he did not take it lightly. He already knew the name for the girl. "I think Sabine is nice."

When the calico looked at him, he told her of the Sabine River, the silver-watered river that divided Texas and Louisiana, a river that ran all the way to the sea. The Sabine. He remembered seeing it long ago when he was a puppy. A good river. Full of moonbeams. Sabine. It was a good name. And with his long tongue he licked the girl kitten in one big slurp. Sabine. She sat straight up and tried it on. The name suited her. She licked her paws and rubbed her ears.

"What about the boy?" asked the calico.

Ranger looked at the little boy cat, at the crescent moon on his forehead. Except for the white-patched moon, the two kittens had been identical at birth. But as they grew, Ranger noticed that the little male had grown one shade darker than his sister, Sabine. In fact, he was the same color as a possum, not so much silver as gray. "How about Possum?" he asked.

"No!!!" said the boy cat. He did not want to be named Possum!

His sister started laughing. "Possum!" He watched as she tumbled over backward, filled with giggles. If that had been her name, he might have giggled too. Possum!

Mama licked his face. She stepped back and looked at him. The moon fur seemed to glow. As she watched, she saw him grab his sister and pull her down into a wriggling ball of kitten fur. She smiled at his puckish ways.

"Ahh," she said. "Puck."

Puck was paws down better than Possum.

Ranger shook his head so that his ears flapped against his neck. "Puck." He let the name sit on his tongue for a moment. The word felt good, quick and clever like the kitten himself. Then he announced it. "Puck." The calico smiled. So did Puck.

Puck and Sabine. A matched set.

# 17

THERE ARE MANY kinds of messages. Some are delivered by wire, some are sent by pony, some are written on a slip of paper and tucked inside a bottle, then set out to sea to hitch a ride in the warm waters of the Gulf Stream.

Trees send out their own messages. Here, in the languages of cottonwood and beech, of holly and plum, they announced the names of this new son and this new daughter.

And deep beneath the old and dying pine, the roots that held the jar vibrated. A son. A daughter. And the creature inside stirred.

Daughter. Once there had been another daughter. *Yessssss!!!!* Grandmother remembered her, a daughter she had loved, loved harder than any other, harder than she loved the night breezes or the brackish bayous or even the man who had been her husband. Harder than that. Oh yes, Grandmother had loved her beautiful daughter. The daughter who had been stolen. Taken from her while she slept. She thrashed her tail against the hard surface inside the jar.

*A priiiiiccccce*, she hissed. *A price will be paid.*

THE SPACE UNDERNEATH the tilting house was native land for Puck and Sabine, the only home they'd ever known. To Puck and Sabine, it was where they snuggled up with their mama and Ranger. It was the country of their sleeping, the nation of their dreams, but it was also a land of constant entertainment, full of interesting items for exploration. Here was the old boot, the leather of it moldy and cracked. Here were the battered wooden fish crates, shoved there long ago and left to rot. Here could be found a variety of bottles and boxes and odds and ends. All places for kittens to hide and climb and tumble. This area beneath the tilting house, the Underneath, was not so large that the calico mother and the redbone hound could not keep a constant eye on them. They both knew that Gar Face would not take kindly to kittens. And they told them, "Do not leave the safety of the Underneath! Do not, under any circumstances, go out into the Open." It was a serious rule.

*You'll be safe in the Underneath.*

But to Puck and Sabine, Gar Face was just the noise they heard as he clomped across their ceiling, he was just a pair of boots that stomped down the steps at night and returned early in the morning. He was a creature of habit. Leaving the house right at sunset, sometimes driving off in his old pickup truck, sometimes heading out on foot, and always returning just before the sun came up.

Most mornings he remembered to feed Ranger. On these mornings, the mother cat waited until she heard him stop moving above them. Then Ranger invited her to join him at his food bowl. She crept out and ate as quickly as she could, looking over her shoulder to make sure the kittens were still asleep. She would feed them later, but first she had to fill her own belly.

Some mornings Gar Face forgot to set out the food, or maybe he didn't forget, he just didn't do it. When this happened, Ranger kept an eye on the kittens while the mother cat slipped away. She was a good hunter. Often she brought home a tasty rat or a peppery lizard. It wasn't really enough for a dog the size of Ranger, but he never complained. It was better than the empty dish. He often watched her go and wished that he could join her, could somehow break his chain, the one that kept him tied to the post beneath the porch.

How long had it been since he had run freely through the forest? He wasn't sure how far his old legs could even take him now, especially the one that was damaged, the one that still carried the misfired bullet, the one lodged in his front leg. Probably not very far. But maybe far enough to catch a squirrel or a raccoon or a rabbit and bring it home for his family. His family. What a family—one old hound, one calico cat, and their two kittens.

TREES OFFER THEMSELVES up readily for homes. They provide their branches for wrens and robins. Skunks and rabbits nest at the feet of their thick trunks. Beetles and ants burrow beneath their barky skins.

But what about the old loblolly pine along the creek? The one that was struck by a single bolt of lightning a quarter century ago? It's only half as tall now, the upper stories have crashed to the ground. Its pulp, once so thick and sturdy, has turned soft, perfect for grubs and insects and other small inhabitants, an occasional vole or salamander.

This old pine has been a home to generations of animal families, mostly gone now. But there is one who is not gone, one who is trapped among the tangled roots.

She is still here.

Here in her remarkable jar.

Here.

# 20

A TREE'S MEMORY is long, stored in its knots and bark and pulp. Ask the trees, and they will take you back a thousand years, before she was trapped in the jar, when Grandmother Moccasin slipped through the branches of the old elms and blackjacks and the shady chestnuts. Even a thousand years ago, the forest was old, and so was she. Her days were filled with the songs of birds and crickets. She reveled in the moon's waxy light and drifted on the soft, cool currents of the waterways. Often, she napped on the broad backs of the alligators floating like logs in the musty bayous. One alligator in particular, the largest of them all.

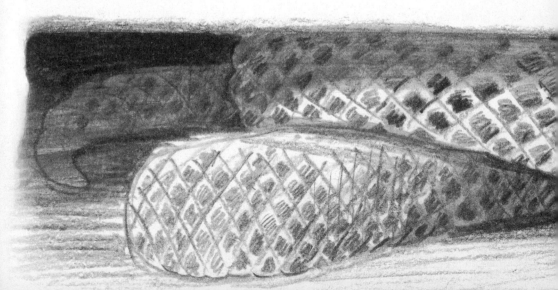

"Sister," he called her. "Brother," she replied. Two beasts of both water and land.

Together they stretched out on the sunny banks of the Bayou Tartine and snoozed in the languid afternoons. He often brought her a salty catfish, and she in turn brought him a swamp hare or a fox.

"I thank thee, sister," he always said, admiring her shimmering scales.

And she, in turn, thanked him, taking note of his bright yellow eyes.

But despite her affection for the Alligator King, she longed for one of her own kind, one of her own species. Here in the swampy forest, there were millions of snakes, both venomous and not. But there were none from her ancient lineage, no other lamia.

Ahh, *lamia*, half serpent, half human.

Blood that ran both cold and hot.

Serpent.

Human.

*Sssssssstttttt.*

Yes, there were humans in this forest, a thousand years ago, the ones called Caddo. Grandmother had seen them in their village alongside the wandering creek. She had seen them gather at the water's edge, heard them sing their songs, watched them dance their dances and hold their children.

Humans.

Grandmother knew about humans.

Hadn't she once fallen in love with a son of Adam? Hadn't she once shed her gleaming scales, so black they looked blue, and donned her own human skin, smooth and tender? Hadn't she handed over her large and generous heart to this man? Once?

A snake's memory is long, and Grandmother remembered. Remembered wrapping her own two arms around her beloved partner, remembered his voice in her ear, remembered the touch of his hand on her back. Hadn't she loved him so much that she had turned her back on her watery family, her reptilian cousins, the creatures of the warm and silvery seas? Hadn't she?

And hadn't he betrayed her? Hadn't he wrapped his arms around another? *Ssssttttttttt!!!!!* She remembered this, too.

The venom rose in her mouth at the thought of it. She had lived in the world of humans and found only misery there. So she had stepped back into her beautiful scales and slithered into the warm Aegean sea, leaving her betrayer and his kind behind forever. And for thousands of years she stayed in the waters, avoided the coasts of Africa and Majorca and the sunny beaches of Baja, the rocky tors of Newfoundland and Wales and the black sands of the Pacific Isles, stayed in the deep, blue seas.

There is a rule: Once a creature of enchantment returns to its animal form, it cannot go back. The rule was fine with Grandmother Moccasin. She would choose her reptile cousins over humans any day. She would remain in the tribe of water moccasins, known for their steel-trap jaws.

Centuries later she spins in her jar and remembers a different man. A man with coppery feathers in his hair. Remembers how he stole her daughter. Her eyes blaze in the unforgiving dark.

Venom pools in her cotton white mouth.

*Sssssssooooonnnnnnn!!!*

# 21

BEFORE A MAN becomes a man, he has to be a boy. Gar Face was a boy when he walked into this forest, a boy whose face was battered and scarred, a boy who left behind the tar-covered wharves of the Houston Ship Channel.

When he first stumbled into the woods wet and humid, every part of him ached. His face ached from the swollen wound placed there by his father. But other parts of him ached too. His legs ached from walking. His mouth ached from thirst. His hand ached from gripping his father's rifle. His stomach ached from hunger.

For days he stumbled through the woods, moved deeper and deeper into the darkness, where the ground puddled beneath his steps and the thick moss hung from the branches like tangled beards on ancient trolls. He did not miss the sun, the way its light illuminated his sorry face, but the unfamiliar terrain ate at him. The sounds of the woods edged their way into his nerves.

Despite this, he moved farther and farther into the darkness.

When at last he stumbled onto the swift-flowing creek, he slipped down the bank and into the salty water, where, despite its brackish taste, he drank and drank and drank. Then he pulled himself onto the creek's edge beneath a towering pine tree.

He tried to sleep, but couldn't. Hunger kept him from it, a hunger that reeked, that oozed through his pores, through his whole body. He had staved off starvation by eating the thin grasses that poked up in the small spots of sunlight, he dug for grubs and worms along the bank. But these were not enough for a growing boy. Yes, he was still a boy. He needed more.

Earlier, he had tried shooting at the small animals, rabbits, squirrels, possums, but he was a poor shot. He had only one bullet left. He would have to find a larger target, an animal that he could not miss.

He leaned against the enormous tree and waited beside the creek. Waited. He braced himself against the eerie cries of the owls and the deep-throated chorus of bullfrogs. He sat as still as the tree itself.

Finally, just as the sun began to disappear, he heard a rustling to the north. Something large was moving toward the creek from the opposite side. Quick and quiet, he waded across the salty water and tiptoed up the other bank. There, right in front of him, not six feet away, was a white-tailed deer, a buck. The deer turned and looked directly at him. For a full second, neither of them moved. Slowly, Gar Face raised the rifle and lined the deer up in his gun sight. Sweat oozed down his face and burned his eyes, but he dared not blink. The deer shook its head and turned away. The boy panicked. "No," he gasped. He could not let this animal escape: He squeezed the trigger and fired.

At the crack of the rifle, a thousand birds rose into the air all around him. But he didn't move. It was a direct hit. He could see the spot where the bullet entered the deer's side, that's how close he was. But instead of falling, the deer took flight. As soon as the bullet hit its target, the buck vanished. Alarm rose in the boy's throat. He could not lose this animal. He could not. He gripped his father's rifle and took off after it.

He couldn't see the deer at all, he could only chase the sound of it rushing through the forest. He could hear the snap of limbs and hurried hoofbeats just ahead of him. He ran. Branches swiped at his sore face, tore into his skin again and again. He stumbled over roots. Prickly vines pulled at his ankles and legs, dug into his pants. Still, he ran.

His heart pounded in a drumbeat of hunger, of pain, of want, of furious want. He couldn't swallow for want of air. Couldn't see for want of light. Couldn't stop for want of want. Here was want crystallized in the shape of a damaged boy. He kept running. His sides ached. Still, he stumbled through the darkness, followed the sound of the crashing deer.

How long did he run? He couldn't tell. An hour? A night? A lifetime? All at once, he hated the deer for running, for taking his last bullet like a thief. Hatred rose in his gut. His insides burned. Once hatred brews up, it spills over. The boy's hatred for the deer became his hatred for his hard-edged father and his runaway mother, hatred for the city he had left behind, until all of it mixed together and turned into a bargain, a bargain struck upon hatred. If the deer escaped, Gar Face knew, he would die himself, die of starvation. But if he won, then he would stay here and stake his claim. That was the deal.

If he defeated the deer, he would rule this place, this God-forsaken pit of trees and water that tasted of salt, this old and forgotten forest. Yes, this place would be his.

The stakes pushed him, drove him. Find the deer or die. He ran on. The dark deepened. All he had left was an empty rifle, a battered face, and the urgency of his very own bet. He quit feeling his aching ribs, he didn't notice the blood running out of his nostrils and dripping into his mouth, or the blisters on his heels. He would run until he collapsed or the deer did. What did he have to lose, who would even notice? He ran.

The deer stayed just in front of him. The night spun, the Earth tilted. He gasped for air. But still he ran, ran behind the flying deer, until at last, the boy, this boy, tripped over a thick root and crashed onto his arms, scraping the skin away in a burst of pain. The rifle slid away from him and landed against the trunk of a chestnut tree.

He lay there for a full moment, the blood rushing in his ears. He couldn't hear the deer. It had escaped. A trickle of blood dripped from his dry mouth. Nothing was left. He couldn't move. He choked up a knot of phlegm and blood and spit it out. Quiet surrounded him, filled his ears. He couldn't even hear his own uneven breath coming in gulps. Finally his breathing slowed.

He closed his eyes. He would lay here until all that was left was bones and the ragged clothes that draped his skin. But then he heard a soft noise only a few feet away. Breathing. Was it breathing? He lifted himself onto his knees and listened. Silence. He must have been mistaken. He sank down into the thick pine needles. He was done. Every muscle in his body screamed. The night felt thick against his skin. Thick and black.

But no, there it was again. Panting. Not his own. He pulled himself up onto his hands and knees and crawled toward the sound. It had to be the deer. Just feet away, he saw its black shape lying on its side, saw the outline of its body in the deep grass where it had fallen, saw the life running out of it. Gar Face took his knife and finished it off.

Tonight, at last, he could eat. He pulled himself up and raised his arms toward the sky. That's when he noticed that he was standing not in the thick forest, but rather in an open meadow. The sky made a dome above his hands, and for a moment a million stars blinked down on him, but only briefly, for in the short time that followed a storm rushed across the forest and obliterated the pinprick lights of stars. A soft rain began to fall. Gar Face sank down next to the fallen deer, and for the first time since he had left his drunken father on the living room floor, he laughed, a harsh and wicked laugh that made the trees shudder. The rain fell and fell, soaked into his weary, jubilant skin.

On the far side of the creek, Grandmother stirred in her deep and lonely prison. She knew all about bargains.

*The prrriiiicccccce!* she whispered. *There's a prrriiiccce.*

# 22

THERE IS HARDLY anything that grows faster than a kitten. It wasn't long before their mother's milk wasn't enough for them. In addition to hunting for Ranger, the calico cat now had to spend more time than ever tracking down mice and lizards and small birds to feed to her babies, too. While she was gone, Ranger watched over Puck and Sabine. The mama cat never worried when her babies were with the hound. She knew they were safe with him.

Twice a day she slipped out from the Underneath and headed into the surrounding forest. Once during the day while Gar Face slept, and again at night after he drove off.

Her calico coat was perfect camouflage in the brown and gray leaves that carpeted the ground; she took care to duck behind the friendly trees and to avoid any open spots. She did not tarry, did not linger in this Open. She would not leave her kittens for long.

*Soon,* she thought, *I will need to teach them how to hunt on their own.*

The idea of it frightened her. When that day arrived, she would have to lead them out from the Underneath, and as soon as she did, they would be perfect prey for any number of hawks, coyotes, and even raccoons. Or worse. Gar Face's image flashed across her thoughts.

*My babies will have to be clever,* she thought, *clever and brave to survive out in the Open.* Until then, she and Ranger told them over and over again. "Stay in the Underneath. You'll be safe in the Underneath."

# 23

BUT BEFORE PUCK and Sabine could be clever and brave, they had to be . . . *kittens!* Here was Sabine, hiding behind the old wooden fishing traps, the same gray color as her coat.

Then . . .

Quiet. Oh so quiet.

Sabine made herself small. Oh so small. As small as a mouse. As small as a cricket. As small as a flea.

She crouched down low. Oh so low.

Her paws tingled. Her ears twitched. Her tail switched.

Patient. Oh so patient . . . until . . . Puck . . .

Unaware. Oh so unaware.

And . . .

Attack!!!

Here was Sabine the mountain lion! Sabine the snow leopard. Sabine the Siberian tiger. Up on her back legs! Front paws raised!

*Hiiissssss!!!*

No matter how many times she did it, she always caught her brother by surprise. Puck's fur stood on end. Then Puck stood on end. The chase was on!

Now here was Puck. . . .

Inside the heavy leather boot, which was deep and very dark, the darkest spot in all of the Underneath.

The smelliest spot in the Underneath.

Sabine will not go in there. Too smelly.

Puck waits. Smells Sabine.

She knows Puck is there.

*Shhh* . . . don't tell Puck.

Attack!!!

It was Puck the pouncer! It was Sabine the pretender!

Dashes. Tumbles. Electric fur. Hisses and spits.

Whew!

For kittens, life in the Underneath was completely perfect.

# 24

GO BACK A thousand years and see Grandmother Moccasin, asleep in the afternoon sun, soaking up its warm rays, letting them sink into her large, thick body. Life for her was perfect too. Or at least it should have been. It might have been if she had not been one thing—lonely.

Singular. She had no twin. She had no mother, at least not one that she could recall. She had no close companion except for the old alligator, and he was not the snuggly type.

All this aloneness wore on her. Go back a thousand years and see. See her gliding among the shadows all alone. See her curled up on the flat rocks of the creeks, lonesome.

"Sister," said the alligator, "your time will come." She knew that he was becoming impatient with her. But it did not alleviate her loneliness. From the bank of the bayou, she watched him sink.

Once in a while, she picked up the scent from the village, the scent of humans. It did not help to know they were near. At night she heard the beating of their drums and knew they were dancing together. Holding hands together. Laughing and eating together. Together. It had been a long time since she had felt the comfort of together. Then she thought of her long-ago husband, the one who had left her for another, and she swished her long tail behind her, a whip.

Humans!

*Ssssssstttttttt!!!!!*

She had no truck with humans.

But she was tired of being alone.

And then one day, while she was basking on the stump of a giant cypress tree, she heard a voice she'd never heard before. "Mother!" Someone was calling her.

She opened her eyes, and there, right in front of her, was a small, beautiful snake, her skin so black it looked blue. She was a carbon copy of Grandmother herself, just as shiny, with eyes as smooth as glass. Grandmother was startled. Was she dreaming? She blinked her eyes. The tiny snake smiled at her. Who was this? Where had she come from?

Grandmother looked back at the little snakelet. She smelled her. Here was such a fresh smell, like clean air after a rainstorm. Here was such a sweet smell, like the foamy waves of the open sea. Here was a different smell from the millions of other snakes that roamed these piney woods. Here was the smell of someone just like her.

Happiness settled on Grandmother's skin and sank into her shiny scales, down through her bones and into her very middle.

"I've been looking for you," the little snake said. After so many years of believing that she was the very last of her kind, Grandmother's heart sang.

"Daughter!" said Grandmother. And the little snake wrapped her small body around Grandmother's chin and smiled.

## 25

SOME MYSTERIES ARE hard to divine. Where does a lamia come from? What kind of parents can spawn a creature who bears the blood of both snake and girl? The animals of enchantment come from long lines of other magical beings. There are those from the sea: the selkies, the mermaids, the ondines. And from the earth: the griffins and fauns, the minotaurs.

Grandmother herself had never known her own origins, so it didn't matter to her where the little snakelet came from. All that mattered was that she was here. Here in this ancient piney woods. Together.

It was a happy time, a sweet time. During the day, they floated just beneath the surface of the clear creeks, dove down to feast on fish and crawdads, filled their bellies. In the afternoon, they clambered onto the flat rocks that jutted out over the salty creek and took in the warm rays of the sun. Sometimes they rested on the back of the giant alligator who kept his home in the large bayou that ran through the darkest part of the woods.

Grandmother called this new daughter Night Song, for though snakes are not known for their voices, Night Song had a gift, a gift passed down from her ancestors, the sirens, those enchanted singers who called to the old mariners on their ships and lulled them to sleep in their hammocks at night, to dream their beautiful dreams. Night Song's silky voice was like those of her great-aunts, lyrical and lovely, and it rose into the air like a bird.

The song of a siren has no words, at least none that anyone can understand, except perhaps the trees, the willows and yaupons and sycamores, but no one else. Likewise, Night Song's singing contained no lyrics, only a pure and soulful melody that wove itself around the leaves and settled into the listening ears of the other forest denizens. It was a lullaby for the piney woods, for all the beings small and large, furred and feathered, scaled and slick. Night Song's lullaby.

Listen.

Here it floats atop the bayou's surface. Here it wafts between the pine boughs. Here, slipping through the damp air.

Listen.

Night Song sang to the crickets and the mosquitoes, to the flowers—the jack-in-the-pulpits, the lady's slippers, the horse-mint and water lilies. She sang for the foxes and coyotes and beavers and minks and bears and wolves and panthers. She sang for all of them. And in return, the creatures of the forest adored the small, beautiful snake. Each night, when she was done, she and Grandmother curled up together in their nest, peaceful and safe.

For many years the two lived happily, and with each passing year Night Song grew more beautiful. Her song more lovely. They might have gone on like this forever, for a snake's life is long. Longer still is the life of a lamia, whose blood is both human and reptile.

Ten long centuries have passed. Now, in the jar, Grandmother hissed, *Sssssstttttt!* Her mouth filled up with poison. Her eyes glowed in their deep, dark bed. And not too far away, the Alligator King opened his yellow eyes and blinked. He had not seen her for a thousand years, did not even know where she was. All he knew was that she would return. Someday, he thought. Sooner rather than later.

Then he sank to the bottom of the Bayou Tartine.

# 26

THERE ARE NO maps of this forest, so thick are the woods, too thick for any cartographer to measure or survey. Only a few, like Gar Face, know the narrow paths of deer and fox and peccaries. Just a handful know the ancient trails of the Caddo, gone now to Oklahoma and Mexico, where the roads are easier to find.

Only those who earn their keep by trapping and skinning the mink and bobcats and raccoons know of a hidden road where a single pickup truck can carry a hard-edged bitter man to an old tavern where the barkeep will offer up something hard-edged and bitter to drink in return for the skins of those forest creatures. Once a trading post for the French, there are still no electric lights, only the yellow glow of kerosene lanterns. In the dark of night, you cannot see this glow from the outside. In the light of day, the bar sits in the shadows. Only those who know it's there can see it.

Gar Face found the tavern years ago. Night after night, he sits in the darkest corner, beyond the circle cast off by the lanterns, his hat pulled down over his face. He doesn't join the few others who know this place, the others who laugh at his broken face.

Instead he waits at his corner table and listens to their stories, stories of elusive black bears and nearly extinct painters. And always, always stories of alligators.

Now, here in this run-down tavern along a hidden road, he sips the black rum that burns as it slides down his throat, and smiles. The hundred-foot alligator of the Bayou Tartine swims through his thoughts as he empties his bottle. He gazes at the other hunters and knows that soon his story will best any that they can muster. Soon.

# 27

RANGER WATCHED THE kittens. Here they were, his Puck, his Sabine. He wasn't their father, true, but he might as well have been. He felt like their father. He did all those father things—he helped them with baths, he fussed at them when they got too close to the Open, he told them funny stories. And what else does a bloodhound do? He sings, of course. But instead of singing the blues, Ranger made up a song just for his kittens, and every night before they went to sleep, he lifted his head and bayed. Every night.

> *Like the sweet moon keeps the sky*
> *Like the wind goin' whooshing by*
> *When those ol' sunbeams break the day*
> *I will keep you while you play*
> *Just as ol' river keeps the fishes*
> *And little stars keep silver wishes*
> *Just as the ocean keeps the blue*
> *I will stand here close to you.*
> *When all around is dark and deep*

*When them ol' shadows slowly creep*
*Even when you're fast asleep*
*It's you I'll keep, it's you I'll keep*
*No need to cry, no need to fear*
*I will always be right here.*
*I will always be right here.*

Here was mostly what the kittens needed: A mother cat who fed them, a perfect place to play, and a hound who promised to watch over them.

# 28

KITTENS ALSO NEED to learn to hunt. The calico cat realized this. Here's a mouse. Here's a lizard. Here's a garter snake. One
by one, she carried these home in her mouth, still alive, and set
them in front of Puck and Sabine.

A new game!

Sabine knew just what to do. . . .

Chase the mouse. Chase the lizard. Chase the garter snake.

She was Sabine the ocelot, Sabine the panther, Sabine the
catamount.

Puck knew what to do too.

Chase Sabine.

# 29

HERE ARE SNAKES. The brilliant green water snakes, the hognose snakes, the corals and rattlers and massasaugas, the copperheads and rat snakes, the kings and garters. Some are shy. Others will chase you. Of this latter, beware the moccasin, skin so black it looks blue, mouth so white it looks like cotton. Other snakes are known to strike in self-defense. But the moccasin, she will latch on and stay there. The moccasin's jaws are like a trap. She can snap a small branch in two, can slice an unsuspecting lizard in half, can sever a finger from your hand, or take off a toe. Beware the moccasin with her cotton mouth.

# 30

DO NOT GET in front of Gar Face and his gun. That was one of the rules.

The kittens were only a few weeks old when they witnessed firsthand what might happen when something got in front of Gar Face and his gun. From the edge of the Underneath, they watched one morning when a rat scurried across the filthy yard, littered with broken bottles and rusted cans, dried skins and old bones from animals who'd trespassed. Just above them, Gar Face leaned against the porch rail, lifted his gun, and *bam*! The rat disappeared.

Do not get in front of Gar Face and his gun. It's a good rule.

Another rule: Stay in the Underneath. You'll be safe in the Underneath.

Rules bear repeating. The beasts of enchantment can don their human forms only once.

Once is all.

Grandmother knew this.

Night Song did not.

## 31

IT'S A FACT that kittens are hard to manage. And these two, growing sleek and nimble, were no different. There is also that whole thing about curiosity. Anyone who has ever known a cat knows that they are filled up with it.

Bones, fur, milk, curiosity. That is what cats are made of.

One morning, while his mother and Ranger and Sabine were still sleeping, still dreaming their pre-dawn dreams, Puck wandered to the edge of the dark porch, right up to the edge of the Underneath where he had spent his entire short life, curled up with Sabine, tickling Ranger's tummy, one morning he walked to that edge, that invisible boundary that separated the Underneath from the Open. So many times Ranger and his mother had warned them: "Stay in the Underneath! Do not go into the Open."

But a cat is built for exploration. All his life, Puck had stayed in the Underneath. Now he gazed into the Open, the sparkling Open, and he wanted to go there. Wanted to walk into the soft air of the morning, wanted that wide space that beckoned him to come out, come out, come out.

He walked back to Sabine and nudged her, but she just rolled over and yawned. His mother and Ranger were snoozing away. Who would ever know if he stepped out for a little bit, just a tiny step, just one toe into the Open? His whiskers tingled. Every kitten hair stood up. His paws itched. His whiskers twitched. His whole body quivered.

Soon the sun began to flicker. Morning. Here it was, a perfect time to *leap* out from the Underneath and right into the yard, into the dim light where he wasn't supposed to go, away from the shelter of the porch, from Ranger who watched him, from his mother who nursed him, from Sabine curled up tight, who was his closest friend, Sabine his sister. He bunched himself up, his front paws right up against his back paws, and then, *jump*, out he went!

Glory, glory, the warm dry sun bounced onto his silver fur. It sank right in. He walked farther into its goldy beams.

For a cat there is only one god, and that god is the Sun. And this cat, little Puck, reveled in its smooth morning rays. His mama and Ranger were wrong. The Open wasn't scary at all. It was perfect. He rolled onto his back and let the sunshine settle on his tummy. One huge and satisfying Yes curled all around him.

He had to tell Sabine! And in one quick hop onto his tiny paws, he ran back toward the Underneath, ran back to get his sister.

He ran, ran, ran . . .

straight into the terrible hands of Gar Face.

*Yeeooowwww!!!*

# 32

IN THE UNDERNEATH the calico cat felt a sudden electric charge zip right through her. She sat up. Wrong was everywhere. She looked around. Found Ranger astir. Wrong, wrong, wrong. Found Sabine, fur electrified. Wrong. Something was wrong. She looked again. Where was Puck?

No no no!

She heard him cry.

No no no!

She bounded to the edge of the Underneath just in time to see her baby lifted into the air by Gar Face.

No no no!

Lifted by the scruff of his neck. She saw his terrified face, saw the bottoms of his tiny pink paws swinging in the air.

"No, no, no," she cried.

And then she did what any mother would do, she ran toward her baby. But with his other hand, Gar Face swept her up as well. Swept them both up, grabbed them both and began to laugh, his laughter ringing through the morning. Here was laughter hard and cruel. He carried them to his truck and stuffed them into a burlap bag, and tied it with a string. Then he tossed them into the bed of the pickup and started up the engine.

Ranger, awake now, fully awake, howled and howled, tugged at his terrible chain. Howled and howled and howled.

No no no!

Gar Face was cruel, but the chain was worse.

The calico cat clawed, she hissed, she struggled. She had to get out of this bag, this bag that smelled of bones and fish and something ancient. But the bag held, the ratty tie was tight. She stopped her fight and held on to her kitten and cried.

Puck felt dizzy, dizzy from the smell, dizzy from the pent-up air, dizzy from being swung back and forth, from the roar of the engine, the hard bed of the pickup. His mother drew him close, close, close. They could hear Ranger howling. Hear the rumble of the motor. Feel the motion of the truck as they drove away, away from Ranger and Sabine and the safety of the Underneath.

It lasted for a long time, the smell, the bag, the to and fro. Ranger's howls grew dim.

The kitten cried. His mother licked his ears, his nose, his face, licked his tiny tail, his pinky paws. The bed of the pickup was hard and cold. At last the truck stopped, and there was a new sound.

"Water," said the mother cat. "We must be near water."

# 33

PUCK SHIVERED. HOW could he tell his mother he was sorry? He was so, so sorry for breaking the rule. He should not have left the Underneath and walked into the Open. He should not have rolled onto his back and soaked up that goldy sun. Instead he should have stayed in that holy darkness, curled up next to Sabine. Where were they? How would they ever find their way back? Where was Ranger? Hadn't he promised to keep them safe? Hadn't he sung that song every single night?

But the mother cat, she didn't wait to hear his sorry. She told him, "I should have known better than to have you kittens in such a dangerous place."

The calico cat looked hard at her beautiful baby, her boy kitten. And right there, tucked beside him in the dark burlap bag, she loved him as hard as she could, loved him so much that her heart nearly burst. "You are the son I dreamed of," she told him. "I never wanted any other son but you." She licked him on the top of his head, right on the crescent moon. And even though her girl kitten was not with her, she loved her, too, held her against that big old love that comes from all mamas, so that surely Sabine knew, she'd know, she'd surely know. And her heart broke for Sabine, her girl cat. Then she gasped.

They say that when someone is about to die, they can see their entire lives pass before them, and that may be true, but some, like this mother cat, can also see the future. What she saw terrified her. She looked at her Puck.

"You have to go back for your sister," the mama cat told him. "If something happens to me, promise you'll find her." His mother's voice was urgent. "Your sister. You have to get her away from Gar Face."

He promised. He did.

And who else did the mama cat love with all her might? Ranger, of course. Ranger with his lonely song and his silky ears. She loved him, too.

"The chain," she said. "Ranger's chain . . . you have to break . . . he'll die if you don't break the cha—" But she didn't have time to finish.

# 34

A PROMISE. PUCK promised to go back for Sabine and Ranger. Promised to break the chain. To a cat a promise is sacred. His mother tucked him tightly beneath her chin, so that next, when it felt like they were flying, they were flying through the air, spinning, he closed his eyes and held on to his mother, spinning through the air until . . . water all around, water that rose up to meet them, seeped through the burlap and pulled them down, down, down.

"Swim," said his mother. She was clawing against the cloth, clawing at the small almost-opening, clawing against the ratty tie. His mouth, his nose, his ears, filled up with water.

"Swim," she said. He pushed his little paws as fast as he could, but he was tangled up in the burlap. The water pulled him down, down, down. He was drifting, drifting, down, down. Swirling. Then he felt a push, a strong push from behind. "Swim." And he did.

Somehow the burlap bag came open. He could see the light above him, see it change, see the wavery air, shimmery through the surface of the water. He could feel his mother right behind him, just behind him, right there, feel her pushing him up, up, up.

He just knew she was right behind him. Right there. Knew it. He could feel her. He could hear her.

"Swim."

Which he did, as hard as he could, in the cold, cold water of the creek. He couldn't see the loose string of the burlap, the single strand that wrapped itself around her paw, couldn't see it hold her, caught in the old mussel beds at the bottom of the deep creek. All he could hear was "Swim."

Puck swam away, his mother's voice in his ear.

"Swim."

# 35

AS THE MOTHER cat's lungs filled with water, as she slipped into darkness, she heard a small voice. "Sister," it whispered, "your baby is safe." Startled, the mama cat opened her eyes and looked back, and caught her breath for just a moment. Saw the radiant sun slipping through the branches of the trees. Ahhh, such warmth.

Then she looked again. A hummingbird!

"He's safe," said the tiny bird.

"Yes," replied the mother cat. She could see that. Her baby was safe. But while she gazed, while she felt the soft glow of the sun, she also caught a glimpse of Ranger and the tiny sister left behind, curled up together in the cold darkness beneath the porch. In the Underneath.

"Come," said the bird, "follow me." But as it is for any mother, she longed to go back, go back to these two, so sorry she was to leave them, how could she leave them? How could she bear to leave the simple songs of such a hound, the tiny purrs of such a kitten? Worry washed over her like a wave. She had to warn them. How could she warn them?

"You can't go back," whispered the hummingbird.

"I know." She sighed. She looked once more at Puck.

What had she done, to put such a large promise on such a small cat? Remorse filled her up. "Oh dear," she cried.

She did not hear the rumbling of the engine as the man drove back to the tilting house, did not hear his hideous laughter slipping through the pickup's window, did not hear the soft-sighing of the trees, only the whispery wings of the tiny bird.

# 36

IT'S THE TREES who keep the legends. Ash, beautyberry, chestnut—they know the one about the hummingbird. They know that the hummingbird can fly between the land of the living and the land of the dead, that she has been known to accompany the spirits to the other side, hover there awhile until they are settled, but then she can return to the side of the quick. That's why she always seems to be in such a hurry, for it's well known that crossing from one side to the other must be done at speeds beyond our seeing. And aren't hummingbirds hard to see? Some call her an "intermediary," and that's a good name for her. Some call her a messenger, the right term too. Some know her as Rainbow Bird, which has nothing to do with her special powers, and everything to do with the way she glimmers in the sunlight.

But mostly? The hummingbird is looking for someone. She's been searching for a long, long time.

## 37

GAR FACE IS not the first human to make his home in these piney woods, nor will he be the last. Long, long ago, there were the people known as Caddo. They made their home along this very creek, this salty creek.

The trees remember them. They do. Many centuries ago, the Caddo crossed the Gulf of Mexico from South America in bark boats and settled here, merged with the Algonquians from the north, the Apache from the west, made their own nation, sang their own songs, learned the ways of the trees and the animals and the wandering streams. Learned how to make jars and bowls and pots from the red clay that lined the creek.

The Caddo can be found in the memories of trees. Not just pines, but hackberries, tupelos, water oaks, winged elms, mulberries, cedars, cypresses, yaupons, bois d'arcs. The trees remember the village by the creek, the creek where the old pine stood. This creek.

It's called the Little Sorrowful, and it flows from a deep, deep well, far beneath the forest floor. It is older than the bayous to the east, the Bayou Tartine and the Petite Tartine. The creek is older than they are and saltier. The salt, it is said, comes from tears.

Most certainly a few of those tears came from a half-drownt kitten. As he pulled himself out of the salty water, with his mother's voice still ringing in his ears, he looked over his shoulder to find her. But all he could see was a hummingbird, hovering just above the water.

That's all.

He looked around.

All his short life, he had never had a moment without someone who cared about him nearby—his mother, his sister, his hound. He had never, ever been alone. Suddenly the enormity of this moment rolled over him and he began to shiver.

Here was one soaking-wet kitten, covered with mud from the streambed. Beside a creek made of tears. And all this kitten could do was cry.

Only a few feet away the old tree stood, helpless, while deep below, still tangled in its roots, the creature stirred. She knew what it was like to lose someone. But unlike the kitten, she did not weep. Instead, she slashed her viper's tail at the solid wall of the jar. *There's a priiiicccce*, she hissed. The jar filled up with steam.

## 38

RANGER'S NECK WAS sore, rubbed raw, from pulling on his chain, and his throat ached. Finally, he curled into the damp darkness beneath the porch. He was bred for scent. The scent of squirrels, of fox, of deer, of possums, of raccoons, of quail and ducks and geese. But right now all he could smell were the lingering traces of his best friend, his calico cat and her tiny boy kitten, his kitten too. All he could hear was the echo of his own frantic bays, now ceased, his shallow breath. He almost forgot about Sabine until she curled up, small and lonely, curled up between his aching paws.

What do you call someone who throws a mother cat and her kitten into a creek, who steals them from the hound who loves them, a hound twisting at his chain wailing, who never even looks back, what do you call someone like that? The trees have a word: evil.

When Gar Face returned to the tilting house, he tugged on the chain, he dragged Ranger out from the Underneath. Dragged him away from the tiny kitten curled up next to him, left her there, silent, trembling, dragged him into the stinking yard and kicked him hard. "Stupid dog!" he shouted. "What good is a dog who can't even keep a cat out of the yard?" Ranger felt the steel toe of the boot grind into his side. He coughed. His throat was so raw that he began to choke. No noise came out.

Normally a hound who has been kicked with a steel-toed boot yelps out in pain, cries in agony. But Ranger was done with crying. He had not a single whisper of a cry inside him. His throat was too raw, his voice was too tired, he could not raise his head to bay a single note, not one. He dragged himself back under the house. He could not cry out loud. But tears splashed onto his silky ears. Sabine, smallest of all, tasted the salt as she licked them.

# 39

LITTLE SABINE. SHE was not as tall or as sleek as her twin. Instead, everything about her was round. Looking into her face, with its silver fur, was like looking at the circular face of the full moon, and when she slept her body was a coil.

Now here was Sabine, alone with Ranger, her faithful guardian. But here also was a sister without her brother, a daughter without a mother. What was left for Sabine?

She looked at Ranger, his chest rising and falling in pain. What could she do? She wanted her mother to come home, to walk into the Underneath with a tasty mouse hanging from her mouth. She wanted her brother to leap out at her from the smelly boot. She even pawed at it, once, twice, thrice, as if with her strokes she could conjure up her silver twin.

More than anything, she wanted to make Ranger feel better. She looked toward his empty food bowl. Her own stomach growled.

Then all at once, she realized: *She* would have to become the hunter. All the small critters that her mother had brought back still alive, all the mice and lizards and grasshoppers that Sabine and Puck had treated as playthings, had taught her something. They had taught her to become the predator that she was meant to be. At this, she sat up on her haunches. With her rough tongue, she licked her front paws one at a time, taking care to polish her sharp little claws. Then she walked to the edge of the Underneath and looked out into the awful Open. Soon she would have to go out there, like her mother and her brother, now lost. She took a deep breath and moved closer to Ranger, his rasping pants filled her ears. Yes, she would go into the Open, but not until night.

Sabine, descendant of the great lionesses of the Saharan plains, grandchild of the mother tigers of the Punjab, tiny heiress of the fearsome lynx and cheetah and panther, night hunters all.

Here was Sabine.

# 40

THE WATER IS not the only element that offers up magical beasts. Look into the upper stories of the trees, look at the tops of the highest cliffs, look into the wispy, whispery clouds. For as long as there have been merfolk, there also have been the great creatures of flight. Grandmother, who had swum the ancient seas, who had been on the murky Nile, home of the scribe Thoth, half ibis, half man, should have known this. She should have known about Hawk Man.

If she had understood the languages of willow, birch, and bitternut, they would have told her about him. Here, in this pine forest. If she could have heard the tales spun by blackjacks and water oaks and junipers, they would have shared his story.

Here, they would say, in that long ago time, was a young hawk, his feathers coppery in the morning sun, his eyes brown with flecks of gold. See him catch the wind currents and fly in wide, swooping circles, see him rest in the tops of the great pines and chestnuts. This piney woods, this great expanse of wetlands, of swamps and bayous, of slow-moving turtles and giant armadillos, was new to him, for he had traveled a long, long way. Here he was, a member of the tribe of feathered changelings, come to make this forest home.

Grandmother Moccasin should have known about the young hawk who nested in an old tupelo tree, right along the banks of the crystal-clear creek, the bird who had listened to the sound of the night, the crickets, the cicadas, the hoot of the owl, the young hawk whose ear was keen enough to hear the rabbit burrowing and the crawdads humming.

This young hawk.

In the evenings, he often sat alone in the trees by the lovely creek. There, he could cock his head and hear the creatures of the night, the owls and bullfrogs, the cicadas and white-tailed deer. Like the trees themselves, he knew the songs of wrens and warblers, the Carolina parakeets, the whip-poor-wills and crows and red-cockaded woodpeckers, for wasn't he one of their kind? Wasn't he?

But he also listened to the songs of the villagers, the ones who lived along this same creek, the ones known as Caddo, who filled their jars with water, who hummed while they did their chores and laughed at the antics of their children. He listened to their voices, too. The part of him that was human coursed in his blood, pulsed with the beat of the drums. He stretched out his strong wings and cried, *"Screeeee!!!"*

One night, when the air was still and quiet, he heard something new. At first he had no idea what it was. Not an insect or a bird, not a frog or a raccoon. Not a member of the village. No, this was different. It was the most beautiful sound he had ever heard. A melody without words. A song without lyrics. It came from the other side of the creek, deep in the darkest part of the forest, toward the bayous, the large one and its little sister, a place where the villagers rarely wandered because of the quicksand and the million poisonous snakes.

He listened.

There it was again. He leaned toward the music as it floated through the thick night air of the forest. The young hawk knew right away that what he heard was a source of tenderness. All at once, he understood its beauty and clung to the clear lovely notes. Night after night he turned his ear toward the song. At first he listened with his ears, but as the nights passed, he found himself listening with his whole body.

Grandmother Moccasin should have known about him.

# 41

A THOUSAND YEARS later . . .
   Here is another listener.
   Puck, wet and cold,
      listening for his mama,
      listening for his sister,
            listening for his old hound, Ranger,
                  listening to the creek running by.
   All he heard was loss.

   Loss. A small, hissing word. A word that simmers into nothing.
Beneath the old pine, Grandmother stewed inside her jar. Loss
engulfed her as it had a million times before in this dark space.
*Losssss!* she whispered.
   A word that scrapes against the skin.

# 42

WHERE WAS GRANDMOTHER a thousand years ago? Swimming through the old bayous, sunning on the rocks beside the creek, sleeping in the drowsy cypresses. And meanwhile Hawk Man listened to the music wafting through the trees. He listened with every cell, every muscle, every copper-colored feather. After so many nights, he knew he had to find the singer of the beckoning song. He flew across the salty creek, past the shifting sands, listening for the sultry notes. He let himself be pulled along on their lovely chords, until at last he found the swampy realm of Grandmother Moccasin and Night Song. He landed in an upper branch of a large cypress and watched the two wrap themselves around the trunks of the tallest pine and glide to the very top. He was sure he had never seen a creature as lovely as Night Song in her shimmery scales, so black the blue of them glowed. He knew he had never felt this way before.

Smitten is what the trees might call it, if they had a word like that in their vocabulary. Birds might have a different word.

The piney woods is known for its birds. Here there are

martins and swifts and flycatchers, ducks and warblers and boat-tailed grackles. When the birds saw Hawk Man, hypnotized by Night Song's melody, they called out to him.

*Brother! Fly away!*

He heard their warnings but paid them no heed. The song he needed was not theirs, not the song of the chickadees or the wood ducks or the cinnamon teals. He needed *her* song.

Together, the cranes and spotted owls, the stilts and king-fishers raised their voices in a chorus.

*Fly away, brother hawk. Fly away!*

But he was not interested in their anxious warnings.

All of them, the vireos and kinglets, the peregrines, their voices grew frantic.

*Turn away, brother. Fly!*

He paid no heed.

Hers was the song that filled him up, wing tip to wing tip. And as he circled the pine forest, the air soft on his feathers, he lifted his own voice, *Screeeeeeeee!!!* And the night sky filled up with his longing.

Most of us would think the song Hawk Man heard was only the sighing of the wind, or the whisper of the leaves in the trees. We might think it was a star tumbling through the atmosphere or the water rushing down the creek. We might guess that a turtle was creeping through the pine needles or an alligator was push-ing his fat feet against the current. There are many things we might think. But only Hawk Man knew what he had heard.

# 43

ANIMALS SING FOR reasons. Coyotes howl to set down the sun. Nightingales warble to please the emperor. Prairie dogs bark to attract a mate. Night Song sang because she was happy.

With her ancient mother, she had learned the mysterious ways of the forest. Grandmother taught her where to find the tastiest crawdads, how to slither high into the trees, all the way into the upper canopy; she taught her where the secret underwater caves lay hidden along the deep sides of the salty creek. No one knew the piney woods better than Grandmother, no one, except perhaps for the trees.

And no one told stories like Grandmother, either. Grandmother told Night Song about the Greek Isles and the white temples that lined the coast of the Mediterranean. She told her about the merfolk of the Irish Sea and the old dragons, their wings glimmering in the sunlight, gone now, long gone. She was careful to avoid her own story, the one of her husband and his betrayal. Why dwell on sorrow, she thought? Instead she shared tales of the whales and albatrosses and all the penguins at the end of the Earth.

No daughter was more beloved than Night Song. No mother more respected. The loneliness that Grandmother Moccasin had known for so many years was long gone. With Night Song, her life was complete. Where Grandmother went, there was Night Song. And where Night Song wandered, Grandmother was close behind. They were inseparable.

But as it is with any child, after a time, Night Song grew restless. She was no longer a snakelet. She had grown into a long and lovely young snake, and like any young woman, she longed for an adventure of her own. Her forest home, with all its mysteries, began to feel small. The tales that Grandmother told so well only made her more restless. And to add to all that, Grandmother began to seem old, older than the oceans and the hills, and she was. Night Song grew weary of so much oldness. She wanted something new.

Day by day, Night Song began to wait until Grandmother closed her eyes for her nap, and she slipped off on her own, just to see what she could see and hear what she could hear.

It wasn't long before she noticed the handsome hawk, his wings broad against the afternoon sun.

Now, alone in her small dungeon, Grandmother hissed, *Betrayed!* Deep beneath the loblolly pine, the one along the old creek, she spun in her anger. *Betrayed. Betrayed. Betrayed.* There is nothing new about betrayal, she thought. Nothing.

# 44

AT SOME DEEP level, we're all of us connected. It seemed that Night Song, while she felt the blood of her strong and powerful mother whom she loved mightily, when she looked up at Hawk Man, handsome in his coppery feathers, his eyes flecked with gold, she also felt the blood of those magical selkies, those enchanted ondines, those lusty mermaids, those lamia from far back in her ancestry. And it was all this blood, enchanted and not, that made her slip down the tallest tree while her mother, the one who raised her and protected her and loved her so well, slept unawares, this blood that led her straight into the wings of Hawk Man.

And like those other legendary shape-shifters, the moment he wrapped his wings around Night Song, she stepped out of her scaly skin and into the skin of a human, a beautiful sleek skin, while he shed his avian form and claimed his own human shape, tall and handsome, coppery feathers in his long black hair, his eyes dark with glints of gold, warm and welcoming.

Here they were, two in brand-new skins, facing each other. Hawk Man held out his hand to Night Song. She took it.

And all around, the watchful trees, the oldest ones, shimmered. They knew that Grandmother Moccasin, when she awoke, would not be happy. The trees knew, but they also recognized the moment for what it was: a love so strong that there was no going back for either one. So for just a little while, the soughing trees used their own ancient magic to stir up the Zephyrs of Sleep. To keep all the others in the forest a-snoozing until Hawk Man and Night Song, in their brand-new skins, had slipped away. For trees, who see so much sorrow, so much anger, so much desperation, know love for the rare wonder of it, so they are champions of it and will do whatever they can to help it along its way.

# 45

A CAT WHO has been nearly drownt needs some time to recover. A cat who has lost his calico mother, who has been taken from his sister and their very own hound, needs a lot of solace.

But first this cat needs to find some food and shelter, especially with the evening drawing nigh. Puck looked around. At his feet ran the awful creek. A shiver crawled down his spine. *Water. We must be near water.* He coughed. He pulled himself up the bank away from its dreaded currents. His coat was matted from the mud at the bottom and along the sides. He was wet and cold. He looked back at the silvery creek and shivered again, then he looked as far upstream as he could. His mother had been right behind him, hadn't she? She was right there, pushing him up, telling him to *swim, swim, swim.* And he had. But when he dragged himself out of the water, she was nowhere to be seen. He looked at the creek rushing by. Where was she? His calico mama? She had been right behind him. He turned around and looked downstream. Maybe she had swum by him, passed him in the tumble of the waves.

As he stared, he saw the water curl around the bend, it hissed against the muddy banks. *Away, away, away* it seemed to say.

And then, right there, on the shore of the silvery creek, that creek full of tears, Puck knew that he would never see his mama again. Never.

It's a soft-sounding word, "never," but its velvety timbre can't hide its sharp edges. Especially to a small cat who has broken the rules and conjured the word in the first place. He sat down hard, soaked and cold. In his deepest bones he knew that no matter how long he stared at the cold water, he would never see his mother again. Never pressed down on him. It grabbed him by the neck and shook him. He sucked in a deep breath, sucked in all that never and started to sneeze. Never filled his nose, his eyes, his soaking fur.

He shivered again, and looked at the opposite shore. Where were Ranger and Sabine? He cocked his ears. Surely Ranger would call for him. If only the hound would raise his voice, Puck would know what direction to follow. He was sure of it.

He sat at the top of the bank. Below him, the creek slid by, the creek that took his mother, the creek that almost took him. He listened for Ranger's familiar bay. But all he heard were crickets and a few evening birds. He shuddered and turned away. And there in front of him was an old tree, dying.

As he approached the tree, he noticed a dark space at its base. Puck went closer. He sniffed the opening. He looked inside. It was small in there, but it was dry. *Stay in the Underneath. You'll be safe in the Underneath.* Those were his mama's words, still in his ears. He had broken the rule. And now she was gone, and he was all alone.

He walked inside. It was cozy and dark, and even though his belly rumbled, he curled up in a wet, muddy ball, and drifted off to a fitful sleep. Never, hard and cruel, settled up against him.

How could he know that deep, deep below him, almost directly below him, in fact, there was an ancient beast, curled up just as tight? She too was asleep in the underneath.

You wouldn't think that these two, one so young and one so old, would have a thing in common, but they did.

Missing.

Yes, missing can happen to the best and the least of all of us. Puck missed his family. Grandmother missed Night Song.

# 46

THE TREES, THE alder and magnolia, the laurel and flowering ash, know about missing. They miss the passenger pigeons and the woodland bison. They miss the panthers and the black bears. They miss the Caddo, who roamed here for eons.

But they also know about revenge. Revenge stays lodged in the memory for a long, long time. For a thousand years.

After Hawk Man and Night Song slipped away, Grandmother Moccasin wrapped herself in a cloak of hatred, wrapped it so tightly around herself that eventually that was all she knew.

Anger and hatred, wound together, have only one recourse. Poison. Poison filled Grandmother's mouth, her cotton mouth. A man had taken the one thing that she loved more than water, more than air, more than the man who had betrayed her so long ago: her daughter. Night Song. Grandmother vowed revenge, a vengeance so bitter it glazed her skin and sharpened her terrible fangs.

She simmered in the darkest part of the piney woods, where the cypress trees towered over the marshes, where the ground was thick with quicksand, where she settled into the nests of Night

Song's cousins, the tribe of cottonmouths. No human dared to enter this part of the forest, and that suited Grandmother, suited her just fine. Here was anger hard and cold, so tight it shut out all the light.

Her eyes grew accustomed to the darkness so that nothing was safe from her. She dined on owlets and mink and frogs, anything that moved or didn't. Her hunger was enormous. She could spot a marsh rabbit from a hundred yards. Her lethal jaws, like scissors, snapped her prey in half. And as her anger grew, so too did she, long and thick, her body as big around as a tree's trunk.

Even her old friend, the Alligator King, knew to give her a wide berth. "Sister," he told her, "choose another way."

But she could not.

"Ssssssttttt!" she said. "Sooner or later, Night Song will be mine again."

The alligator closed his yellow eyes, heaved a heavy sigh, and sank to the deep and muddy bottom of the Bayou Tartine.

# 47

GAR FACE FOUND the old house one day when he was out coon hunting with Ranger—back when they were both much younger, before the accident that made Ranger lame—stumbled upon the house that even then tilted to one side. Who knows how long it sat there, abandoned? There was no lightbulb and no running water. But Gar Face needed neither. Nor did he need a mailbox or a telephone.

Few creatures in these woods even knew that Gar Face was here. No one in the old hidden tavern ever met his eye and he made no attempt to meet theirs. He simply sat in his dark corner and drank his bitter brew. No coins were ever exchanged. Only skins. Skins that he hung on the porch rail of this tilting house to let them dry.

This house. This tilting house that sat perched on a spit of high land where he parked his truck, where he could curl up on the old cot that served as his bed, where he could come and go in his own way and time and no one would be the wiser. Where he could throw his trash into the yard, and who would care? Where he could use the old outhouse without closing the door because there wasn't a door anyway.

Usually it's better for a house to be inhabited. There's something about the moisture in a person's breath that restores old wood and gives the place some dignity. A house with people who live there tends to sit upright on its moorings. Usually that would be the case. Maybe this house sat for too long before Gar Face moved in. But if you looked at it from just a few feet away, if you could get close enough without Gar Face aiming his rifle at you and snarling like a wolf, you would swear that it was sinking into the ground of its own accord, as if the only way to escape from its terrible inhabitant was to disappear into the earth.

# 48

SABINE WAS THE witness. She had awakened just in time to see her brother step into the sun's dim light, see him roll onto his back, see the beams of the sun float onto his tummy. She had seen him smile up at the lovely light, seen his coat glow in the shimmery gold. She started to step into the shimmer with him, even though she knew he was breaking the rule, the rule about the Underneath. But just as she called out to him, there was Gar Face.

She witnessed Gar Face as he snatched up her brother and then her mother and stuffed them both into the brown burlap bag, watched him throw them into the back of the pickup truck. She had tried to tell them, tried to warn them, but her cries were lost in her brother's cries, her cries had matched his and so sounded like only one.

She witnessed the truck drive away. She witnessed the dust, the mean and swirling cloud of dust that curled around the back tires and filled the air.

She witnessed the trees shivering as the truck disappeared from her sight, carrying her mother and brother. And as if all that wasn't enough for one tiny kitten to witness, then she watched Ranger tug against his chain and howl as if his heart was breaking; his heart *was* breaking, she knew. She witnessed it. Saw him pull and pull and pull against the chain. Saw him yelp and cry and howl until he had nothing left, until his neck was raw and bleeding where the chain dug into the skin, rubbed the fur away and left it bleeding, raw, sore, until he had no voice at all, until he couldn't utter a single sound.

She witnessed Ranger as he dragged himself back underneath the house, the house that tilted to one side, the house that smelled of bones and flesh and something rotten. Underneath. And all she could do, all that was left, was to curl up beside him, beside the hound, her beloved hound, the one who had sung to her even when she was still inside her mother. She curled up beside him, licked his silky ears, and purred. That was all she could do.

Her mother was gone. Her brother was too. But she had Ranger. And she knew that they had to get away from this place, the only place she had ever known. Even in her smallness, she knew that Ranger would not last much longer tied to that chain.

# 49

MEMORY IS A slippery thing. When something terrible happens to you, like the loss of someone you love, like the loss of a mother or a father, or perhaps a twin sister or an old hound, memory can turn into a soft blanket that hides you from the loss.

But this was not the case with Puck. No. He remembered. Soon, he would have to figure out how to keep his promise to his calico mama. Soon, he would have to find Ranger and Sabine. Soon, he would have to eat!

His belly rumbled. He had not eaten anything for a whole day and night. All he had ingested was water, lots and lots of water. He sat up and stretched. He licked the fur on his left side and got a mouthful of dried mud. He spat it out. His coat was caked in it. All at once, he felt trapped by the dried bottom of the creek, encased. He had to get it off.

For the next hour, he tugged and licked and rolled. The mud was like concrete in his fur. When he pulled at it, tufts of fur came out with it. *Ouch!* He started to panic.

He tugged and licked and rolled some more. Finally he began to cry again. His skin itched, his mouth was dry, and he was still a mess.

He lay down in a heap and wept. Wept for his silver fur, coming out in patches. Wept for his missing mother and sister and hound.

At last, spent from so many tears, he pulled himself up and looked around. He had cried so hard that now he was full of hiccups. Puck had been hungry before, but now he was starving. Mouthfuls of dried mud do not satisfy a hungry cat, especially one who is growing despite his travails.

Everyone knows that a cat is built for stalking, for tracking its prey and pouncing. He wished that he had paid better attention to the advice of his mother when she had brought home the mice and lizards and voles for himself and his sister to practice on. "You'll need to know how to catch your own one day," she had told them. Sabine had taken her seriously.

But for Puck, they had been a game. Lizards especially provided hours of amusement. He loved to bat them into the air and catch them with his front paws. It had all been loads of fun. But now, his belly rumbling, his skin itchy, he was not interested in playing. Trouble was, the key to stalking any kind of prey is silence.

Hiccups are not silent.

He tried holding his breath.

*Hic!*

He tried lying on his back.

*Hic!*

He felt like crying again, but he knew if he did, he'd simply have more hiccups. A cat with hiccups cannot sneak up on anything. A cat with hiccups is a sorry sight.

## 50

IN THE WELL-kept records of trees, would you find the joining of Hawk Man and Night Song a thousand years ago? Yes, the magnolias and blackjacks and beautyberries, they would tell you that here were two who had turned their backs upon their own kind.

Together these two searched for a place to settle. They walked on their unfamiliar legs and feet until they were weary. They followed the paths through the woods, paths made by deer and bears and bison. They camped along the sluggish bayous. They traipsed all the way to the edge of the forest and beyond, where they gazed upon the wide and beautiful river to the east. It was lovely, and for a while they thought they might stay there, along its sandy shores. But without the shelter of their beloved trees, they felt vulnerable.

More than anything, they felt alone. Humans are designed to be with other humans, even those with mixed blood. They need each other's laughter. They require each other's sorrows. They are made to swim and cook and hunt and gossip together. Mostly, they need each other's stories, stories of love and wisdom and mirth. Hawk Man and Night Song needed other humans. And so they turned away from the slow-moving river with its open skies and the tall grasses that grew beside it and walked back through the forest, back across the open meadow and all along the animal paths to the village beside the creek. The Caddo village.

Once there, the people welcomed them as their own, as Caddo, and they sang and danced and celebrated this new arrival, made Hawk Man and Night Song members of their tribe. There are mysteries about the Caddo, but one thing is known. They were a welcoming people, open and friendly. The young couple found a family. And right there, in the village alongside the creek, they built a hut of branches and mud, a home.

Ask a tree and it will tell you about homes. Ask the old loblolly pine and it will talk about how it offered up one small den for one small cat. And deep below, trapped in its dying roots, one beautiful old jar for an old, old snake.

## 51

HAPPINESS WAS THERE in that small hut beside the creek, and soon enough Hawk Man and Night Song bore a baby, a little girl. All babies have a glow about them, but Hawk Man was certain that his daughter glimmered. The trees welcomed her right away, just as they do all babies.

And Hawk Man?

When a young man becomes a father, the sky above him, the ground beneath him, the rising and setting sun, all become something new, as if he's never seen them before, as if this little daughter has turned everything all at once into a huge and wondrous Hello. When Hawk Man held his baby girl against his chest and looked into her tiny round face, he felt a love so deep he thought he might drown. It scared him a little, this new kind of love. It was different from the love he felt for Night Song, not more or less, just different, protective and humbling.

When he looked down into his daughter's dark eyes, she squinted at him. Then, in an action he'd never forget, she raised her tiny arm, uncurled her fingers from her plum-sized fist, and touched his chin. She looked at him with such seriousness that Hawk Man was certain that she was trying to tell him something. He could only wonder what it was. Then all he could do was kiss her tiny fingers and smile.

## 52

NIGHT SONG ALSO loved her little daughter. She held the baby close, just under her chin, and nuzzled the girl's fine silky hair. She breathed in her baby-girl smell. Rubbed her fingers along her baby-girl skin. On her baby-girl head, Night Song planted a million kisses, maybe more.

Even though Night Song was still new to the village, the people there had welcomed her. If you could know the Caddo, you would know that they were master potters, and it didn't take long for Night Song to learn this craft. While her daughter slept, Night Song made bowls of wonder, jars for keeping seeds and nuts and corn, bottles for water, for crayfish, for juice made of the small black dewberries that grew in the open meadows. She even made jars for burials, funerary jars meant to accompany the dead to the other side so that they'd have something for carrying their food and water, something to present to their relatives waiting for them, a gift.

On these jars, she always drew a hummingbird. For it was well-known, even then, that the hummingbird was the one who took the dead to the other side and then came back. Night Song knew this. And so did the villagers. And also the trees.

If you could see the jar that held Grandmother, you would not find a hummingbird etched on its side. You would not.

# 53

IF IT WEREN'T for Ranger, Sabine might have left, might have waited until the dark rolled under the house and over it and slipped away, into the woods beyond the yard where she had noticed the yellow eyes of others blinking in the dark. She did not know who or what those yellow, blinking eyes belonged to. Perhaps they were simply fireflies, for fireflies tend to hang along the edges of woods. A less rational being than Sabine might say they were haints with their dim lanterns, blinking on and off. These woods were full of haints, or so it was said. Sabine did not truck with old ghost stories. She knew that haints kept to themselves.

She looked out at the blinking eyes, for that's what she knew they were, not fireflies or haints, but simply the other animals of the piney woods, the night animals, the raccoons and foxes and rabbits who came just to the edge of the filthy yard, and she dreamed of walking away with them, of leaving this awful place.

But she would not leave Ranger. One day she would figure out how to unfasten the chain, and they would leave this God-forsaken house with its terrible tenant and never look back.

# 54

GAR FACE ALSO knew about haints. Ever since he had seen the Alligator King, he wondered if his mind was playing tricks on him. Had he really seen a hundred-foot-long alligator? Did such a creature exist? The possibility of it ate at his insides.

Night after night, he pushed his old pirogue up and down the Bayou Tartine, his kerosene lantern threw a circle of yellow light atop the muddy water. It was impossible to see more than a foot below the surface of the whisky-colored drink; the murkiness made a silty curtain that hid the inhabitants below.

Nevertheless, the warm light was inviting, especially to mosquitoes and moths. It wasn't unusual for a small brown bat to wing into its circumference, snapping up the insects. Gar Face had no quarrel with the insects and the bats. He brushed them away from his face as he peered into the brackish stew. Where was the beast?

Gar Face had come a long way from that unskilled boy who shot the deer so long ago. He was no longer a terrible shot, but a good one. He could trap and skin anything, even snakes. Only the bobcat had escaped his predatory skills, and that was the dog's fault. Not his. But it was the alligators that drove him. Only the alligators challenged him, matched him wit for wit, only the alligators gave him a run for his money. The other animals were no match for his scheming and riflery. No, the gators were a different story. Fierce and cold. Worthy opponents.

As well, it was alligators that paid the biggest price, the skins of their bellies turned into purses for women who attended plays in New York and London, turned into supple boots for men who wore silk socks and did not tramp through the marshes and woodlands, turned into briefcases for executives who sat at satin-finished desks and looked out onto taxi-choked streets. Alligators, same as gold.

But it wasn't gold that interested Gar Face. It was something bigger than gold. It was seeing their faces, the men who looked away when he walked through the door of the old tavern on the hidden road. The men and their stories, each trying to outdo the other.

Faces. He sneered. Their faces would be as ugly as his when they saw the skin of his hundred-foot gator. He knew they'd curl their lips in an ugly shock of surprise. Greed and jealousy made people ugly. *Yes*, he thought. It was bigger than gold.

He drew deeply from his bottle, felt the warm liquid slide down his throat and settle into his stomach. He knew that the alligator was here. He could feel him. Could feel the old creature lurking, just beyond the cast of his light.

"I'll find you, brother," he said, under his breath. "Count on it."

A hundred feet below, the Alligator King smiled. And when he did, a million bubbles floated to the surface, rocking the pirogue above. Gar Face reached down to catch the edge of the boat with his hand. He looked over the side into the water.

If he had looked instead at the lantern hanging on the bow, he might have seen the hummingbird hover there, just inside the light. Might have seen her. He might have been even more surprised than he was already by the rocking of the boat. Since when did a hummingbird fly through the night?

Something big was beneath his boat. He was sure of it. He took another swallow from his flask.

## 55

PUCK.

Itchy.

Frustrated.

Hungry.

Sad.

*Hic!*

Could life be any worse? As if it could, he felt a flea on the tip of his right ear. He scratched it with his back paw.

He couldn't seem to stop the itching, the sadness, the frustration, or the hiccups, but he could try to stop the hunger. He stepped to the opening of his little den and looked out. It had been a long, lonely night. The sun was just coming up. Ahh, the sun. For a brief moment, he remembered its goldy gold. Sunk into its warmly warmth.

But just as quickly, he remembered the trap he had walked into. He looked out at the gentle rays, sifting through the treetops. How could something so sweet be so dangerous?

*Stay in the Underneath. You'll be safe in the Underneath.* He retreated back into his dark den.

Fear washed over him. The sun was so inviting. Just as it had been the day before. All glittery and warm. All cozy. But hadn't the sun betrayed him? Hadn't it lured him out from his safe space and led him right into a trap?

Suddenly a new emotion entered the picture. Anger!

From somewhere deep inside him . . . *hisssss!!!* Then it happened again. *Hisssss!!!* All that hissing made him feel better.

At once he knew what to do. He would scare the sun! He took a deep breath and let out his most ferocious *HISSSSSSSSS!!!* All the fur on his back stood up. He looked back out the opening. The sun had not budged. It was still gently casting down its rays, warming up the trees that surrounded him. How could one small cat with matted fur scare the sun? He plopped down on the dirt and peered out. He could almost hear Sabine laughing at him. Sabine. Where was his sister? Where was Ranger?

He took a deep breath.

Then he took another.

What was this? It seemed the hissing had undone his hiccups. For a tiny moment, he felt a little proud of himself. At least he had conquered the hiccups. He sat up a little straighter and took another breath to be sure. No hiccups. But the moment of satisfaction was swift. His belly still ached. And all that dried mud had also made him thirsty.

He lay there for a long time. As he did, the sun grew brighter, his stomach grew emptier. He began to feel dizzy from hunger. Soon, he knew, he would have to leave this den and find something to eat, and he did not think he could wait until it got dark again. He gathered up as much courage as he could muster and stepped outside. Sunlight bathed him from top to bottom. It sank into his matted fur. Maybe this sun, this warm and goldy sun, wasn't so bad after all, and for a second he felt a little sorry about hissing at it. Just a little. He took another deep breath, without a hiccup, and was glad for those hisses.

Once outside the den, his ears filled up with strange noises. When he had lived beneath the tilting house, there were only the noises of his familiars—Sabine's purr, his mother's voice, the stomping of the man's heavy boots, the grinding of the old pickup's motor, Ranger's howl.

Where was Ranger? Why didn't he howl? Where was the voice that could lead him back, back to the Underneath? He listened as hard as he could for Ranger's howl. He had no idea how far away he might be, or even in which direction to listen. But surely Ranger would call for him?

He sat very still. New sounds filled his ears. Cheeps and chirrs, chatters and clicks, all the normal sounds of a forest. His mother had told him about them, about the birds and insects and chattering squirrels.

He listened. But then he heard something else . . . was it wind? The breeze in the treetops? He looked up, but the trees were still and quiet. He turned toward the sound. What was it? He walked toward it. Then he froze.

The creek. Of course! The creek was only a few feet away. A small jolt ran down his matted back.

It wasn't the sun who was the enemy. It was the water! He should go as far away from the creek as he could! But then he stopped.

The creek!

The creek was the answer. Somehow he knew that the creek had something to do with his way home.

Home. Puck looked over his shoulder at his small, dark den. It was safe and dry. There was plenty of room for him to sleep, and it had a fresh smell to it that the tilting house did not. But here was no mama. Here was no Ranger. Here, no Sabine.

On ginger paws, he crept out. Out into the light. Then he stepped closer to the edge of the creek. Just below him was the salty Little Sorrowful, tumbling by. He looked across the water to the other side. From his sunny spot on the bank, the other side looked dark, unwelcoming. Sabine and Ranger were over there. How he knew, he couldn't tell. He just did.

*Go back. Go back. Go back.*

His stomach grumbled.

*You have to break the chain.*

He closed his eyes and listened to the water rolling beneath him.

*Promise you'll go back.*

Deep beneath the old tree, Grandmother tucked her nose underneath her long body. *Ahhh, promises,* she thought. She knew about promises. *Sssssstttt* . . . she had made one long ago. She spun in her jar. Spun a web of promises. She knew about promises. There was always a price.

## 56

LET THE TREES take you back. A thousand years, to the deepest, darkest part of the forest, the forest on the other side of the Little Sorrowful Creek, where the big and little bayous brewed in their marshy beds. Go there and see Grandmother Moccasin, see how she simmered in her anger, year after year, day after day. After Night Song ran away with Hawk Man, Grandmother's vitriol grew along with her girth Years passed, and she grew. The poison in her mouth became more toxic. Finally, on the tenth anniversary of that fateful day, the day that Hawk Man had taken Night Song from her, she made a decision, a decision that had been growing for ten mean years. "I've waited long enough," she said out loud.

From her perch in the knotted cypress, just beside the larger bayou, she called to her only remaining friend, the alligator.

"Brother," she said, "it's time."

From the murky waters of the bayou, he floated to the surface and blinked his yellow eyes, eyes that looked like the sun. He turned his gaze to her with a solemn stare. "Sister," he said, "you must be certain."

"Of course I'm certain," she retorted. She had talked many times of her plan to lure Night Song back to her. She had dreamed dreams of the two of them climbing into the branches of trees, exploring the underwater caves, dining on crawdads and catfish, basking in the sunlight that warmed the soggy forest floor in patches. She had dreamed this dream so many times, she could taste it. As if to prove the point, she flicked her long tongue along her bottom jaw.

"The consequences are dire," the Alligator King reminded her.

*"Sssssstttt!"* she hissed. "I know what the consequences are." Of course she did. She knew that if Night Song returned to her serpent shape, she would never be able to don her human skin again. It was a rule that suited Grandmother Moccasin just fine.

"Does Night Song know this?" asked the alligator.

Grandmother did not answer the question. The only thing that mattered was having her daughter beside her again. That was all.

The Alligator King looked at her, but she turned away. He spoke once more. "You must tell her before she makes the choice."

"Enough," said Grandmother. "I'll tell her when the time is right." And with that, she slithered down the cypress tree and began to make her way toward the other side of the forest.

But as she slid away, she heard the alligator call to her.

"Promise you'll tell her before she makes the choice." Then he closed his eyes and sank to the muddy bottom.

"I promise," she whispered. But no one, not even the trees, believed her.

## 57

HOW CAN A cat keep a promise when he is hungry? The good news is that cats are built for the hunt. Their strong back legs are made for springing. Their sharp claws are designed for hooking. And their pointed teeth are perfect for the bite. And now that he was done with the hiccups, he could do a considerable amount of sneaking up. With all this gear and talent on paw, it seemed as though Puck would have no trouble tracking down some breakfast.

He had, after all, watched Sabine prey upon the lizards and mice that his mother had brought home for them.

Hadn't he?

He set out.

For the rest of the morning, he sniffed for mice, skinks, anything that moved. But after several hours, the only thing he had managed to drum up was a pair of crickets that jumped right in front of him, surprising the living daylights out of him, but also turning into a crunchy albeit not very satisfying snack.

The truth of the matter was this: In those practice sessions under the tilting house, he had to admit, Sabine had done much of the serious work of trapping, leaving the remains for Puck. Of the two, Puck could see that his sister was the better hunter. How could he know that in the world of cats, it's often the female who leads the hunt? Sabine was only being true to her forebears, those lionesses, those tigresses, those female ocelots.

Sabine. Thinking about his sister brought a different kind of ache. Before all of this, he had never been more than a few feet away from his twin. The pang grew more taut, as though a string were being pulled from the top of his head to the tip of his tail. They say that the knot between twins is tighter than any other. That twins are so closely bound they can see each other's thoughts, their hearts beat at exactly the same time, not even a second's difference. And once apart, twins come unraveled. Besides being hungry and itchy, Puck felt unraveled.

Missing rolled over him like a thick cloud. Missing Sabine. Missing his mother. Missing Ranger. The pang grew and grew.

He stepped into a patch of sunlight and lay down. In the warm afternoon sun that soaked into his itchy skin, he thought hard about those times his mother had brought home the small gifts that now seemed so large. He traced in his mind how to lay low, he thought of Sabine crouching behind the old fish traps, waiting for an unsuspecting target to run by, then leaping out at just the right moment. He replayed these actions over and over.

He lay in the light, remembering, when suddenly he noticed that the sun had slipped away. He felt a cool shadow drift over him. A chill ran through him. Then he noticed how quiet it had suddenly become, as if the forest around him was holding its breath.

He looked on the ground to see if he could tell where the sun had moved. He walked toward another patch of goldy light, but as soon as he got there, it also went away. Was the sun playing a trick on him? Was it angry about the hissing? He looked for another patch and when he saw the light, he bunched up his back legs and . . . jumped!

Jumped just in time to avoid being grabbed by an enormous bird! Yikes! Puck ran, ran fast, ran as hard as he could to the safety of his den. *You'll be safe in the Underneath.* The bird swooped after him; Puck could feel the air behind him being stirred up by its enormous wings. He slipped into his lair, but he turned around just in time to see the giant bird peering in at him, its eyes gleaming.

Puck took a deep breath and . . . let out his most piercing scream. *YEEEOOWWWW!!!* To his surprise, it worked. The bird flew away.

There are many birds of prey in the piney woods—the owls, the peregrines, the red-tailed hawks, and even the tall-legged waterbirds, the great blue herons and sandhill cranes. Puck could not identify this one.

All he knew was that it was large. He tucked himself against the farthest side of his den, back, back, back, as far from the opening as he could get. There he hunkered for a long, long time, wound into a tight ball, and panted. How did he know that the bird wasn't waiting for him, just as Sabine had waited for the lizard behind the fish traps? It could still be out there. Waiting. The thought of it made Puck tremble. His sides heaved in and out.

But after a while, his body grew tired of being so tightly wound. His legs began to ache from the tension. His ribs felt sore and his mouth was dry from his quick pants. And once again, his stomach, still empty despite the earlier crickets, rumbled. He could not cower in the dark forever. He stood up and tried to shake off the nerves. He had to go out sooner or later or he would expire in this small, dark space. Slowly he stretched his achy limbs and crept toward the opening. Once there, he poked his head out and cautiously looked all around, to both sides and overhead. Day was coming to a close, and the woods were filled with shadows. Still there was no sign of the bird. He stepped out, his whiskers on high alert. He sniffed the air.

He did *not* smell bird.

He *did* smell mouse.

There, right in front of him, just outside his door, was a freshly killed mouse. Evidently when Puck let loose his high-pitched scream, the bird had startled and dropped the mouse.

Even though Puck knew the mouse was already dead, he decided to kill it again, just to make sure. He thought about what Sabine might do. So he fluffed up his fur as much as he could what with all that cakey mud, arched his back to its full kitten height, and pounced on the lifeless body with all four paws. He batted it from side to side and tossed it into the air. He hooked it with his deadly claws and chomped down on it with his sharp teeth. At last, satisfied that he had killed it completely and thoroughly, he took the tail between his jaws and dragged it into his lair and ate and ate and ate. No mouse had ever been more tasty. He ate every little morsel, including the fur and bones, until all that was left was the very tip of the tail. He belched and then he ate that, too. While he ate, he thought about his sister, the hunter. What was she eating this night? Would she take the place of their mother and leave the safety of the Underneath to hunt for herself and Ranger? Puck licked his chops. It was a very fine mouse. He hoped that Sabine was eating a meal as filling as this too. Sabine. He wished he could have shared this mouse with his one and only sister. He would have gladly given her the larger portion. Gladly. Finally, his belly full, he curled into a ball and fell fast asleep.

From a branch in a nearby winged elm tree, a solitary bird watched, its dark eyes aglow in the encroaching dusk. Then it spread its coppery wings and flew away.

# 58

GO BACK A thousand years, go back. In the village along the creek, time passed quickly for Hawk Man and Night Song. Hawk Man, with his ability to listen, had become one of the elders, a man who grew in wisdom, a man who knew the ways of the forest and the seasons, a man who could tell when a storm was approaching or when the buffalo were migrating. The people of the village turned to him for advice and friendship.

He was not one of them, but they loved him nonetheless. Night Song became known for her beautiful pottery as well as her mysterious, wordless songs. The children especially loved to hear her sing as they drifted off to sleep.

Together, Hawk Man and Night Song watched their little daughter grow. In the years since her birth, she had shot up straight like her father, and handsome like her mother. In almost every respect, she was exactly like the other children in the village. Except for one thing.

If the sun shone at just the right angle when it fell upon her skin, she appeared to glimmer.

As the girl's tenth birthday approached, Night Song decided

to make her a special jar, a jar of her own. "Our daughter is becoming a young woman," she told her husband, "and a young woman needs a jar of her own." It would be a fine large jar. A jar for gathering berries and nuts and crawdads, a jar for storing corn and water. It would be a worthy jar for a worthy daughter.

The next day Night Song walked to the edge of the creek and gathered the thick red clay into a basket. Then she rolled the clay into long coils with the palms of her hands and wrapped the coils around and around onto themselves until they formed a shape. Next, she dipped her fingers into water and rubbed the coils together until the surface was smooth, both inside and out. When she was satisfied with its smoothness, she pressed her thumbnail into the surface near the rim. She smiled. The print was a perfect crescent moon. A new moon. She thought of her daughter and smiled. A new moon. A new year. She rubbed her finger over the tiny moon. Then, with her thumbnail, she pressed more and more small crescent moons in a swirling pattern all around the upper part of the jar until there were exactly one hundred. A hundred crescent moons. When she was done, she set the jar on a flat rock and let it dry in the sun.

As the sun began to set, "Time to fire it," she told Hawk Man, and together they gathered the wood for the pit, struck the flint that started the flame, then waited for the fire to grow hot-hot-hot. They lowered the raw jar into the pit and waited. Waited for the fire to do its work, to seal the clay so that it would be impenetrable from either side, in or out.

The fire burned and burned and the pot slowly hardened. Hours passed until at last the flames ebbed, glimmered, and died away. When it was cool enough, Night Song lifted the jar out of the pit, turned it around and around in her hands. It was large and heavy. She felt its weight as she lifted it onto her shoulder and leaned her ear against the smooth surface. Then she set it on the ground in front of her, and with a mussel shell, she began to etch a design around the large bottom, beneath the crescent moons.

She closed her eyes and let her hands lead the work, turning the jar as the shell dug into the side. Hours passed. Her hands worked.

To Night Song, who had spent most of her life without fingers or hands, they were still a mystery to her, as if they had a knowledge all their own. Her eyes still closed, she smiled. Those hands worked and worked. More time passed, until at last her arms ached from balancing such a large vessel. Her fingers cramped from pressing the shell into the hard surface.

When at last she opened her eyes, she was stunned. The carved lines curled around the pot, ducking in and out of one another, and wrapped themselves into a body.

"Mother!" Night Song cried. She fell backward at the sight, landing hard on the ground behind her. The etching on the jar was unmistakable, the long curving body of a snake, the perfect diamonds of the scales moving with the contours of the jar. The etched snake swam beneath the hundred crescent moons.

"It's beautiful," proclaimed Hawk Man, and it was.

Night Song, still surprised by the drawing, stammered, "Yes." She caught her breath. "Yes," she repeated. She looked again at the graceful figure of her mother. "She is." A glint of longing flickered behind her eyes. The appearance on the jar sparked a small yearning to see her ancient mother, the one who had cared for her when she was smaller than her own daughter. She shook her head. Where was Grandmother, she wondered? She smiled at the thought of her. Then, still smiling, she returned to the jar.

To finish the gift, Night Song made a lid, a tight-fitting lid, one that sat snug in the rim. Good for keeping things out. Good for keeping things in. Hawk Man held the jar while Night Song added the finishing touches.

How could they know that even at that moment, while they admired the jar, a jar made by a mother for her daughter on her tenth birthday, just at that very moment, a thousand years ago, Grandmother was on the move?

# 59

OF ALL THE denizens of the piney woods, a kitten falls into the realm of "smaller animal species." In the days that followed Puck's encounter with the bird, he also came nose-to-nose with a large raccoon, as well as a very smelly and noisy peccary. In both cases, he was able to surprise these creatures with his loud and threatening screeches.

*YEEEOOOWWWW!!!* The sound of it split the air. Both the raccoon and the peccary turned around and hightailed it. If they had looked over their shoulders, they would have seen Puck running too, in the opposite direction. Nevertheless, the little cat realized that besides his claws and teeth and springy legs, high-pitched screaming could be a useful weapon.

It didn't take long before Puck learned to use all his tools. In the area near his den, he soon discovered the best places for trapping mice and lizards. Once he even found a mole, sticking its head above the earth just as Puck happened by. And eventually he garnered the courage to walk down the bank beside the creek and lap up the clear water. It was salty, but he drank it. And after he finished, he sat beside the water and watched it rumble by. He was done with being hungry and thirsty.

Now what he had to do was get across that creek. Ranger and Sabine were on the other side. He was sure of it. From above it, at the top of the bank, it didn't look so wide, as if maybe if he took a running leap he might be able to jump over it. But here at the edge, where his toes touched the cool water, where the temperature was lower and the ground was softer, when he looked across it, the other side might as well have been another continent and the creek itself the ocean.

He stared at the other bank. And as he did, he saw a flash of light, like a small rainbow, hovering at the edge. The hummingbird!

He blinked and she was gone.

# 60

ALL OF US have favorites. The sky has favorite comets. The wind has favorite canyons. The rain has favorite roofs. And the trees? Because they live such long lives, their favorites change from time to time. But if you could ask a longleaf pine or a mulberry or a weeping willow, they will tell you that a thousand years ago, it was Night Song they adored. Yes, Night Song and her beautiful lullaby. They loved her from the moment she arrived.

As she stood next to the fire pit, Night Song looked hard at the jar she had made. She had thought of Grandmother many times, and whenever she did, she also thought of the long hours they spent floating on the backs of the alligators, hunting the crawdads in their underwater caves, twisting their long bodies around the tallest branches of the trees. Night Song looked up. She cupped her hand over her eyes to shield them from the bright sun that slipped between their leaves. For a brief moment, she thought the branches were waving to her. Now longing, sharp and keen, pierced through her human skin like a knife, and she caught her breath.

All these years, she had missed Grandmother. But she had

turned her back on the missing, had refused to consider it. The missing was too big to carry around. But now, here on the surface of the beautiful jar, the perfect likeness of Grandmother shone, a reminder that there was someone else besides her husband and daughter who loved her.

A thousand years later, a small cat sits beside this same creek and misses his drownt mother. He misses his silvery twin. He misses his winsome hound. Yes, missing is all around.

# 61

BENEATH THE TILTED house, Ranger stirred. It was dark out, and all he could hear was the chirping of crickets and the quiet rise and fall of Sabine's small purrs as she slept. He licked the top of her head with his big, slurpy tongue. He watched her as she stretched and rolled over. Then she kept right on sleeping.

Ranger got up and crept out into the filthy yard, littered with years of broken bottles, and also the old bones of the beasts that Gar Face had shot with his rifle and skinned on the porch. Ranger had cleaned his share of these bones himself. He licked his jaws. It had been a long time since Ranger had gone on the hunt, had feasted on fresh meat, had shared a fresh possum or a raccoon or a swamp hare with Gar Face. He had been the best dog in the forest, and Gar Face knew it, a dog descended from generations of prized hounds, hounds raised right on the silver Sabine, the wide and silver river to the east of this forest. Ranger had served his master well, had scouted out the beavers and the deer and the raccoons. Once he had even cornered a rare black bear, possibly the only one left in this dark forest. Gar Face had rewarded the dog with steak carved from that very bear.

Only once had the hound paused. Only once. The bobcat. She had stepped out in front of him and stared directly at him. At first Ranger couldn't figure out why he had paused, he only knew that the cat was staring him down with its yellow eyes. Ranger bayed, but the cat kept staring. He stopped and in an instant, Ranger knew. Kittens. This cat had kittens.

He lowered his head. He shifted his stance. The cat escaped.

Now he was lucky to get a bowl of scraps from his master, the man who put the chain around his neck and left him there. The old bullet in his leg burned.

Ranger tugged at the chain. His neck was still raw from pulling against it earlier. And his side ached where Gar Face had kicked him. The chain was taut, it dug into his fur and skin. This chain. This rusted old chain. This chain that bound him to a twenty-foot circle.

While the calico cat had been with him, he had hardly noticed this chain. And now, tugging against it, he was reminded of his lost friend, the best friend he had ever known. And Puck, too. His boy cat. What had happened to them?

And the trees that circled the tilting house, the ones that had watched this old hound for such a long time, who had loved his bluesy notes, lowered their branches and sighed.

# 62

FOR A WHILE Gar Face had been happy with the dog, the one he stole from a farm somewhere to the east of here, near the Sabine River. He was glad for the company, and the hound proved to be a worthwhile companion, a partner in the hunt. True to his master, happy to be out in the open, tramping through the marshy forest, their own swampy kingdom. They were alone in the forest, a solitary man and his faithful dog.

But there came that night when the two of them cornered a bobcat. The dog was baying at the top of his lungs while Gar Face hurried in to make the kill. But just before he pulled the trigger, the stupid dog moved in front of his rifle, allowing the cat to slip out of his gun's sight. Gar Face remembered that night, the cat's eyes gleaming in the dark, all teeth and razor-sharp claws, claws that slashed at Gar Face's leg as it flew past, leaving a stinging gash down his calf. Gar Face yelled. He didn't care that the dog had taken the bullet in his front leg.

Any other person might have felt sorry, so sorry, for an accident like this. But Gar Face was not another person. As far as he was concerned, the dog had betrayed him when he stepped between his rifle and the bobcat. So he chained the stupid hound to a post and left him there, left him in the filthy yard as a reminder.

Do not trust a living soul.

Do not.

# 63

THERE IS NO village along the creek today, but a thousand years ago, there was. As she slithered toward its round huts, Grandmother pushed back the anger that she had harbored and concentrated on the many good times that she had enjoyed with her daughter. *Ahhh*, she thought to herself, *soon we'll have those good times again.* And the thought of it made her move more quickly, as quickly as an enormous and ancient snake could move. *Ssssooooonnnnn*, she hissed. And the watching trees trembled.

Meanwhile, in the village, as Night Song beheld the etching on the side of the jar, the one of Grandmother Moccasin, she was filled with longing for her mother, the one who had cared for her and raised her. How could she know that this very mother was on her way to meet her?

The next morning, she gave the jar to her daughter. It was a huge jar, larger than any she had ever made. It was almost as large as the girl herself. Indeed, if the girl stepped into it, it would almost come up to her chin.

Her daughter wrapped her arms around it, and she could only

barely touch the tips of her fingers around the largest part, right around the middle.

"Oh," she exclaimed, "I've never seen anything so beautiful." Then she turned and rubbed her hands along the smooth exterior. Night Song stood quietly as her daughter carefully ran her fingers across the hundred crescent moons pressed into the upper rim. Then, she held her breath as the girl traced the shape of Grandmother Moccasin. Night Song was sure that her daughter began to glimmer as her fingers followed the curves and scales of her ancient relative. Then suddenly the girl stood back and asked, "Where? Where is Grandmother?"

She had heard only bits and pieces about Grandmother Moccasin. Talking about Grandmother seemed to make her mother sad. But today, the day of her tenth birthday, the girl wanted to know more.

Night Song paused. She was slow in answering; then she told her glimmering daughter, "Grandmother knows all the secrets of the creeks and the trees and the bayous. She's lived here for a long, long time."

The girl listened intently. Then she asked, "But where is she? Where is Grandmother Moccasin?"

Night Song hesitated, then told her, "Cross the creek to the other side and walk until you get to a place where the ground is so soft, your footsteps will fill with water. Go, and go some more. When you find the place where the cypress trees grow in the middle of the water, where the moss drapes down like curtains so thick they shade the sun, where the land shifts and sways, there you'll find Grandmother." She watched as the girl patted the etching of the old snake.

Then, for some reason she couldn't explain, she told her glimmering daughter, "No one knows the forest so well as Grandmother. If you are ever lost or need her, she can help you," and in her heart she believed this. She watched the girl hold the jar away from her to gaze at the carving on the side.

Here was her very own daughter. Her heart's desire. A girl made from a love so deep between herself and Hawk Man that Night Song had abandoned Grandmother Moccasin, the one who had taught her the ways of the forest, had shown her the turning of the seasons, and filled her head with stories.

At that moment, her own child by her side, Night Song felt a rush of gratitude. "Thank you," she whispered. And the trees and stars and water, the whole world, shimmered.

# 64

WHILE NIGHT SONG held her young daughter and opened her heart wide, Grandmother approached the Caddo village. When she reached the other side of the creek, the serpent paused.

She caught her breath. Even though she had never seen Night Song in her human form, she would have recognized her anywhere. There were the eyes, set wide apart. There was the hair, so black it looked blue.

She was beautiful in her human form.

Grandmother hissed. *Ssssstttt!!!* The memory of another human appeared to her like a stab, the man she had given her heart to, the one she had embraced so long ago. He had robbed her too. And now here was Night Song, ten years in her human skin, bound to a human man. *Ten years*, she thought. All that time, she had waited for Night Song to return. She could wait no longer. Anger coiled itself inside her like a knot. She whipped her long tail back and forth, back and forth.

Immediately, she started to charge across the creek to wrap herself around Night Song and tug her down into the waters of the creek. But wait! What was this? Grandmother did not expect to see another, did not expect to see a girl. Who was this?

As she watched from the opposite bank, watched Night Song embrace the small girl, she blinked. The girl glimmered. There in the sunlight, the girl's skin shimmered in a myriad of colors, red, green, blue, indigo, yellow.

"A daughter!" she said. Then she smiled. For she recognized the ancient lineage in the girl's glowing skin, the old blood, the enchantment. *A daughter.* She stopped for a moment to consider this new bit of information.

Grandmother knew she could not *force* Night Song to return to her serpent shape. Night Song had to do it of her own choosing. She had to come willingly. As much as Grandmother wanted to coil her enormous body around her and drag her into the water, unless Night Song came of her own accord, she would simply drown. Now she would have to convince Night Song to leave not only Hawk Man, but this daughter as well.

As she paused, the words of the alligator ran through her mind. *Does Night Song know the consequences? Does she know that if she steps into her viper skin, she can never be a human again? Does she know this?*

*Pish*, thought Grandmother. It made no difference to her whether Night Song knew the rule or not. The only thing that mattered to her then, the only thing that had mattered to her for all these years, was getting Night Song back! She cared not at all about the promise she had made to her friend, the Alligator King.

She did not see this as a betrayal on her part, only a necessity. She would do whatever she could to reclaim her daughter.

She looked across the creek again. There. There was Night Song. There was the girl. And one more. Hawk Man!

*Sssssssstttttt!!!*

# 65

THE WORLD IS made of patterns. The rings of a tree. The raindrops on the dusty ground. The path the sun follows from morning to dusk. Soon a pattern emerged to Puck's life.

In the mornings he awoke in his cozy den at the base of the old pine and waited for the first light of dawn to creep into the opening. Then he quickly walked to the edge of the creek for a drink of water.

After his morning hunt, he found a patch of sunlight for napping, followed by another hunt, and then another nap.

Hunt. Nap. Hunt. Nap. Finally, at the end of the day, Puck crawled back into his den and curled up for the night.

There is a certain amount of comfort in patterns, for they offer up a feeling of safety. Each evening when Puck settled into his small lair, he waited for the deep, deep dark of night to create a blanket, and then he fell asleep. He knew that the reliable sun would wake him in the morning, and the trusty dark would lull him to sleep in the evening.

But one night, after only a few hours of sleep, he rolled over and blinked. There was a light outside the door of his den.

151

Had the sun come up early? Had it changed colors? If the sun came up at a different time, was it a different hue? Instead of goldy gold, did it turn into silver?

Most cats would recognize the moon for what it was, but this cat, Puck, had never been outside at night when the moon began its own cyclical pattern. Always, when night rolled in, Puck had either been underneath the tilting house, or curled up in his little lair.

The silver light peeking into Puck's door was inviting. Usually there is no comfort in surprise. But this different kind of light, different from the yellow light of the sun, seemed to beckon him, and he realized he wasn't afraid at all. He stood up and stretched and walked outside. There he caught his breath. All around, the forest glittered with a silvery cast. Puck looked up. Through the branches of the trees, he could see the pale beginnings of a new moon in the shape of a crescent. If he could have seen his own reflection, he would have noticed that the small patch of white fur on his forehead glowed.

He walked to the side of the bank and looked below at the tumbling water. It was full of tiny moonbeams, dancing on its surface. Even the other side of the creek, normally so forbidding in its darkness, was coated in silver light.

As Puck watched, he noticed a dark shape moving along the water's edge. His fur stood up. He should run. He should hurry back to the den. But then he realized that the animal, whatever it was, was on the other side of the creek. He sat down again and continued to watch. As the dark shape moved closer to the water, Puck noticed that there wasn't just one, but two, then another.

As they got closer to the water, the light from the moon illuminated them. Possums! Of course. Puck had seen possums before. Wasn't he almost named after them? Now here was a large one and two smaller ones, a mother and her kits.

In the silvery light of the crescent moon, Puck watched the three gather at the water and take deep drinks. Then he saw the mama sit back and begin to groom herself while her babies played. He watched the two splash each other and rumble and tumble together. For a long time they played like this, they chased each other back and forth, up and down the bank, then they grabbed each other in a hug and rolled into a big ball together, over and over. Once in a while, they ran in a big circle around their mother. Finally, done with her own grooming, the mother gathered her babies up and started grooming them. Puck watched as she licked each one from nose tip to tail tip.

Suddenly his own mud-caked fur felt itchy. He scratched the back of his ears with his hind paws, but it didn't help. He rolled on the silvery ground. What he needed was his own mother's rough tongue, he needed his sister's tongue to reach the spots on the back of his neck, he needed Ranger's slobbery tongue to give him a good bath.

That's what he needed.

He needed his family. He looked down at the silvery water and knew his mother was gone, but knowing didn't make his need for her go away. Then he looked up, at the far bank. Where, oh where, were Sabine and Ranger? Weren't they worried about him? Did they miss him too? Why didn't Ranger call? Why didn't he lift his voice into the air and sing his bluesy song? If only Ranger would howl, then Puck could find them.

On the other side of the creek, the mother possum finished up her chores and bundled her babies close to her side. Then he watched them walk away, back into the deep, dark forest.

And somewhere, in the middle of that forest on the other side of the creek, Sabine walked out from underneath the tilting house and looked into the night sky. There she saw the crescent moon. It hung in the middle of the inky blue and gleamed.

Puck, she thought. It reminded her of Puck.

## 66

ANGER HAS ITS own hue, its own dark shade that coats everything with a thin, brittle veneer. If Grandmother had not been so
consumed by anger at that moment a thousand years ago, when she
looked across the creek and saw Night Song and Hawk Man and
their little girl, the three of them standing together in an embrace,
she might have seen something different, something sweet.

Someone wiser than Grandmother might have recognized this
old stirring for what it was, the familiar affection that a grandmother feels for her grandchild, an affection as ancient as the trees
and wind and stars. At that moment, she could have turned
around and returned to her dark lair on the bayou, content with
the knowledge that her daughter was well and happy. She could
have left them in their happiness. She could have reveled in
their warmth and quietly whispered good-bye. She could have.

She could have chosen love.

But Grandmother had forgotten how love felt, and so she did
not recognize it when it rolled right over her. Instead, when she
saw Night Song, encircled by her family, all she felt was hunger,
hunger to have her daughter all for herself.

She curled her massive body up in an enormous coil, like a giant spring inside a watch, completely wound, and waited to strike.

On the village side of the creek, the threesome, arm in arm, walked away, away from Grandmother Moccasin.

"I'll wait," she said. And she did. Grandmother waited.

Soon the sun began to set, it dipped below the trees. The ink blue sky filled in the gaps between the branches and leaves. Grandmother waited for the campfires of the village to flicker, to go from flames to embers. Waited for the stars to peek through the thick branches of the watching trees. She waited and waited. She had waited for ten long years, and she could wait awhile longer. She began to hum. From the back of her cotton white mouth, she emitted a low hum, so deep that even the small red wolves, with their ears tuned to lower frequencies, could not hear it, could not feel it. The bullfrogs, known for their low notes, took no notice. Only the snakes, the rattlers, the massasaugas, the corals and copperheads, only they heard Grandmother's hum, only they knew what it was.

Grandmother took a deep breath and hummed again. And she watched and waited. And hummed. All around her the vipers gathered, slid up the trunks of trees, crawled underneath the ferns and fallen logs of the dark side of the forest.

*Come to me*, she hummed. *Come.*

And they did. Whole tribes of them, including her own adopted tribe, the moccasins. There they watched.

*Ssssiiiisssstteeerrrr!* they called. *There's a prrriiiicccccce! There's always a price.*

*Yessss!* she hummed. *A prrrriiiiiiiccce!* Then she closed her ears to them and concentrated on the one she had come for.

Finally, from her spot on the opposite bank, Grandmother saw a lone figure walk toward the creek.

A buzz zipped through her long body, each scale glowed. *Yesssss!!!*

It was Night Song. Grandmother watched as the young woman knelt beside the creek and dipped her hands in the cool water, watched as she let the water sift between her fingers, watched as she dipped her hands again and held her face in her cupped palms and ran her fingers along her face. It was so dark, all she could see was her silhouette, but it was enough.

Grandmother curled up on the bank. She began a chant, at first barely audible; but as she intoned the words, the chant grew stronger:

> *Come to me, my lovely daughter*
> *Step into the silky water,*
> *Slip out of your foreign skin*
> *Don your diamond scales again.*
> *Come my sleek and wondrous daughter.*
> *Come.*

When she finished, she took a deep breath. This was not just any chant. It was one known to the ancient shape-shifters of the waters, the mermaids, the ondines, the lamia: an invisible rope, a lasso that pulled her daughter to her, one magical word at a time.

The trees knew it for what it was, an enchantress's call, but anyone still awake in the village beside the creek might think what they heard was the breeze gliding through the branches, making the pine needles clatter against one another. They might think there was a white-tailed deer browsing in the nearby meadow. If they cocked their ears, they might think a small group of scissor-tailed flycatchers was skimming through the breathless air.

But Night Song was not just anyone in the village. In her veins ran the blood of all her enchanted ancestors, the waterfolk of legend, and there, standing on the bank of the creek, her heart beat like a drum, a wild and ferocious drum. In her ear, she could hear her reptile cousins, the massasaugas, the rattlers, the tiny garters.

*Daughter*, they warned, *there's a prrriiiicccce!*

She paused. Was it a warning? Perhaps she should go back, turn away. The forest seemed to hum.

*Beware, beware, beware.*

The sound of it was urgent. She recognized the copperheads, the hognoses, the orange and black corals. Her sisters. Her brothers. She stepped toward the creek.

*Turn back!*

They filled the air with their steam-filled remonstrances. The creek swirled at her feet, pushed itself against the sandy bank. Even in the darkness, she could see the gleaming water. And then she heard the chant again.

*Come to me, my lovely daughter. . . .*

"Grandmother!" she gasped.

And while her husband and daughter slept in their hut in the village, Night Song stretched her open arms toward the creek. She hadn't seen her mother in ten long years. For all that time, she had pushed the memory of her to the back of her thoughts, there but not. And now here she was, calling to her.

In an instant Night Song remembered her childhood, remembered swimming in the silted bayous, sunning on the back of the old alligator, hunting for crawdads in their underwater caves. She remembered those nights, coiled in the top branches of the trees, remembered the stars blinking at her, remembered.

Grandmother.

Beloved Grandmother.

She was filled up with Yes.

And without a second thought, Night Song stepped into the water.

# 67

ONCE IN A while, Puck caught the glimmer of the tiny hummingbird. She was always a surprise. Here one moment, gone the next. Occasionally she came to his side of the creek and circled his tree. (This was how he thought of the tree now, as his.) He used it to sharpen his claws. He relied on its cool shade. He rubbed against the bark to help get the caked mud out of his fur. He even marked it with his own Puck scent.

Puck's tree, this old loblolly pine, despite its numbered days, knew that his kitten, (for that is how he thought of Puck now, as his), this kitten needed to cross the creek. And when one tree knows something, the others do as well. Where there is a chorus, as there is with a stand of trees, there is a lot of knowing.

If Puck knew the code of the winged elms and wax myrtles, the blackjacks and chestnut, he might hear them tell of the Bayou Tartine and its little sister, the Petite Tartine, of the land between that was made of quicksand. He might heed their warnings: *Stay out, little brother, stay out. Beware the Tartine sisters!*

Puck looked at the old forest on the other side of the creek. Sabine and Ranger were over there. Underneath the tilting house. He had to find them. He had promised.

# 68

PUCK WASN'T THE first one the trees tried to warn. There have been others. A thousand years ago, they tried to warn Hawk Man. They tried.

As soon as Night Song stepped into the creek, Hawk Man awoke. He sat up and rubbed his eyes. How long had he been sleeping? He shook his head, groggy. In the nighttime's dark, he waited for his eyes to adjust. He stretched his arms and yawned. Across from him, his daughter slept, the jar his wife had made beside her. He smiled.

Then he noticed the unused mat beside him where Night Song normally slept. The emptiness was enormous.

He looked at the quiet mat, cold and undisturbed. A stab of panic, like a knife to the ribs, pierced his chest, sharp and quick. Night Song. Where was she? He felt a cry well up in his throat, but he stuffed it back, afraid he might alarm his sleeping daughter.

Quickly he left the hut and ran to the edge of the creek. He walked first upstream, to the bend. There, the weeping willow dipped its fingers into the cool water. He knew that his wife often came here at night to wash her hair. But now, as the salty water tumbled by, there was no sign of her.

All at once, he heard a whirring in the air and looked up. Birds. Birds everywhere, lifting into the dark sky, thousands of them. He listened for a message, but their voices were silent, only the thrumming beat of their wings against the breeze. They filled the dark air, shadows against the sky. Hawk Man's heart raced. This couldn't be good.

He retraced his steps and walked downstream, past the village. He splashed into the creek and stood in the shallow water of the edge. He looked at the opposite bank, toward the thickest part of the woods, thick with brambles and vines and the poisonous ivy that curled around the trunks of the towering pines. His heart pounded. Surely she did not wander into the dark side of the forest, not there. Its large pits of quicksand could swallow up an unsuspecting creature—a deer, or a black bear. Once he and the whole village had witnessed a bison, up to its belly in the sucking mud, struggle for more than a day to escape. Its thick cries had been terrible and deafening. Finally the sand won and pulled the beast under.

Bereft at the disappearance of so much food, Hawk Man had cried for the loss, but to get near the beast would have meant certain death for anyone who tried. They would have gone under too, pulled by the struggling animal and the sucking mud. Helpless, he had stood and watched the great creature disappear.

The memory of the bison set Hawk Man to shaking. He had to sit down. Where was his beloved wife?

He didn't know that there, in the realm of the Bayou Tartine with its little bayou sister, someone else was crying. Night Song. She knew that Hawk Man was looking for her, could feel his presence in the air of the thick and heavy forest. But she could do nothing, only turn her eyes to the sky, to the sight of a host of silent birds, but none of them were her husband, the one who had given up his wings for her.

Here is a woman who has stepped out of her human skin and donned her serpent body. Here is a woman who has gladly followed her mother, the one she loved so dearly, so openly, the one she trusted. Here is a woman, cloaked in a scaled skin so black it looks blue, so shiny it gleams. But here also is a woman who did not know that once she returned to her serpent shape and slid into the water, she could not ever go back to the world of humans. Never.

Here, yes here, is a woman betrayed. Deceived by someone she loved. And so here also is a woman who has forsaken her husband and her daughter forever, the two she loved most. The ache of it has stitched its way through her long, sinewy body, inside, outside, a searing thread that pulled her into a hideous knot. She writhed against its tension, until at last, spent, she curled herself around the branch of an old cypress and listened, listened to the silence of the trees. For what can trees say in the presence of such sorrow? All they know to do is stand, somber and sad.

Below the branch, in the thick water of the bayou, the alligator looked at Grandmother with his golden eyes, eyes like the sun, and said, "You did not tell her."

Grandmother did not have an answer. Instead she spun her massive body around and around in the water, stirring up the silt from the bottom, turning the water into a chocolate cloud that reeked from the rotting leaves and branches that settled there, now churned into a mucky stew. There was no sorry here.

She had Night Song back, didn't she? It didn't matter at all whether her daughter was happy right now. In time she would forget all about the man, the man whose voice rang through the forest and hung on the thick, wet air.

# 69

TREES ARE THE arbiters of time, gathering up the hours and days and years, keeping them in their circular rings. They know that forgetting is not so easy. The blackjacks, the water oaks, the sumacs, they all had time to spare, and more. And they remembered. They remembered the glimmering girl, daughter of Night Song and Hawk Man. They remembered that awful morning.

Here she was, almost ten years old. Only a moment in the life of a tree. Here was a daughter whose father had held her in his strong arms since she was a baby, a girl whose mother sang to her every single night.

The trees remember her waking all alone in the darkness of her family's hut. Was it the aloneness that woke her? She lay very still and listened. She could hear her father calling from a distance, but she also heard something else. What was it? She lifted herself onto her elbows and held her head up so that she could listen better. It could have been wind. No, not the wind. It could have been rain, an early morning rain? Not that, either. Then she recognized it: a sudden beating against the air, the winging of thousands of birds in flight. She looked around. The sun had not come up yet, it was still dark.

Normally the birds did not rise up until daylight. What had caused them to stir like this? And why were they so quiet? All she heard were the wingbeats, none of the regular chatter of birds, the calls of grackles and orioles and gnatcatchers. Why didn't they sing?

At first she thought she was dreaming. The sound of wings filled her ears. Then she heard her father's voice. Both were nearby and far away, close and distant, her father, the birds. The air must be thick with thrashers and wood ducks and kinglets. She opened her eyes and listened. Who was her father calling? Why were the birds so upset? She sat up, the day was barely present, just a thin stream of pearled light in the open doorway. It was early. Then she heard the birds again, circling high above their village. She sat up on her mat and looked around the hut.

Her father. Missing.

Her mother. Gone.

She was alone. All alone. A small thread of fear crept up her back. She had never awakened alone before, without Hawk Man or Night Song.

Wrong filled up her small body and tugged at her. Wrong. It curled up at her feet. Wrong was here, it was everywhere.

Suddenly Hawk Man's voice shot through her skin and bones and pulled her fully awake. All at once she realized her father was calling for her mother. She looked at the unused mat where her mother should have been. Where was she? What had happened to her?

Outside, the sky was thick with birds. Their wingbeats thrummed in the heavy dawn.

She could hear her father.

Over and over he called. The girl clapped her hands over her ears, but they did not erase the sound of his urgent voice. Did not erase the flapping of wings that circled overhead. Over and over her father called out her mother's name. Night Song. Where was she? What had happened to her? The girl rose from her mat and looked out. The sky was overcast, streaks of red bounced against the early clouds and slipped through the limbs of the trees. Dawn. Birds. Silent birds, everywhere, filled the sky. She looked toward the creek. Her father's calls came from that direction. He called and called for her mother, over and over. Something was wrong.

Wrong was here.

Wrong sat on the ground in front of her.

Wrong kept the birds from singing.

Wrong.

It crept up her legs and into her chest.

She heard her father again. Something must have happened to her mother. Her beautiful mother, the one who held her in her gentle arms, the one who sang to her at bedtime. Mother. Where was she? The girl turned and looked at the enormous jar, the one Night Song had made for her just the day before. The birthday jar, its hundred crescent moons pressed into the rim. She lifted it up. She could not leave the hut without it, not this jar. She wrapped her arms as far around it as she could. It was heavy, and she struggled with its weight.

*Hurry*, she thought, *I have to hurry.* And she walked out of the hut with the jar in her arms, its smooth round surface pressed hard against her chest. It felt cool against her skin. She walked as fast as she could, but the weight of it slowed her down. She had to be careful not to stumble and drop it. Oh, glimmering girl, do not drop this jar that your mother has made you. Do not. She stepped quickly, carefully, one foot in front of the other, toward the creek.

The birds circled overhead. She heard them dip and dive above the low clouds and through them. The jar grew heavier with every step.

Finally, she neared the water's edge, where she could at last set her burden down on the soft sand. She took a deep breath and looked below, into the tumbling gray water. Along the banks she saw the red clay, the same clay that had offered itself up to make the jar.

Her birthday jar.

She looked at it, at the strong sweep of its curves, the certainty of its design, the beauty of its etching, the etching of Grandmother Moccasin.

Once more she heard her father call. Call for her mother.

Wrong was everywhere.

In the sand beneath the jar.

On the surface of the water.

Amid the million wingbeats of the birds.

Where was her mother?

The little girl, the one who glimmered, began to walk back and forth along the water's edge, looking and looking. Her mother was here, somewhere, she had to be. The girl could still hear her father's voice coming from the forest. Why were the birds so unhappy? The water swirled beneath her.

She looked back at the jar and as she did, a tiny beam of light fell across it, illuminating the etching of Grandmother. Here was a jar made with love from a mother to a daughter. Here was a jar of beauty. Beautiful like her mother, like the birds, like the etching of Grandmother Moccasin.

Suddenly the sun slipped behind a cloud, and the light on the jar flickered out. Wrong welled up inside of her. "Mother!" she cried, and her cry filled the forest, rang across the creek and through the leafy branches, sliding over the watery ground of the brackish marshes. "Mother!" It rang through the treetops and over the dark water of the bayous, it slid over the feathers of the silent birds. Again and again she called, but her mother didn't answer. Finally she stopped and looked at the whirling water just in front of her.

There was something in the soft mud. Familiar. True. Her mother's footprints. She knelt beside them. Yes, she was sure of

it. Her mother must have walked into the creek, right here. Right here, where the creek bent away from her, where the water lapped the edge and tumbled away, away, away. These, she knew, were her mother's tracks.

Then she stood up and called again, only this time the one she called for was her father.

# 70

NOT TOO FAR away, Hawk Man paused. Someone was calling him. At first his heart raced. Was it Night Song? The voice
was similar to hers. Yes, his wife. She was calling him, he knew it,
he had to find her. "I'm here!" he cried. "Here!" He listened
again, listened for Night Song's voice. Only silence. All he heard
was the circling birds. He knew they were keeping watch, but
their presence brought no comfort. He cupped his hands over
his ears. Which way had the call come from? He stood very still.
There it was again, the voice. A small voice, calling.

His daughter! His daughter must be awake. He had left her all
by herself. Alone, without her mother or her father. Hawk Man
abandoned the forest path and ran back toward the village. He
could hear her clearly now, calling for him. He heard the fear in
her voice. Run, he thought, run to your glimmering girl, run to
your little daughter all alone. Run.

When he emerged from the woods, he saw her standing on
the bank of the creek, her skin shimmering, birds like a halo in
the air above her. His heart broke at her smallness. So small,
this radiant daughter. Quickly he scooped her into his arms,

this small and glimmering girl, this daughter of his and Night Song's.

Wrong was everywhere.

Nesting in the morning air.

Settling on their arms.

Inching up their backs.

Here, right here, on the bank of the creek, stood a father, holding his little girl, her skin glimmering in the morning light. And here is a little girl, hanging on tight. Both of them here, with the silent, circling birds.

When at last neither one of them could hold on to the other any longer, the girl took her father's hand and led him to the place where she had found her mother's tracks. Hawk Man looked down. Yes, there were his wife's footprints. But what he saw right next to them made him step back. "No!" he cried. He gripped his daughter's hand tighter, and screamed, "Noooooooooo!!!"

There, beside the prints left by his wife, was the S-shaped imprint of a snake.

## 71

THIS FOREST IS older than any history, it predates the dinosaurs and mastodons and the giant ferns that touched the sky with their pointed fingers. It's older than old. But even from the earliest times, not long after the old sea herself pulled away from the land and slipped into the Gulf of Mexico to the south, there have been cats. If you only knew the languages of trees, you'd hear about them. The saber-toothed tigers with their teeth as sharp as scimitars. Here they roamed for thousands of years, bearing their young in the thickets and using the ferns as dens. All of them are gone now, only a few fossils remain.

And then came the sleek panthers, the jaguars, the margays. Mostly gone now too, slipped away to other forests, hurried south to Mexico, away from the hunters and poachers who sought their fur for coats and hats. Even the bobcats are few. And the painters, rarest of all.

The trees especially miss them, the jaguarundi and ocelots and pumas. Trees love cats. Whenever a tree has an itch, it can count on a cat to give it a good scratching. Trees love a cat's sharp claws. Love their purrs when they rub against their trunks. Love to hold them in the forks of their branches while they sleep the day away.

No other animal can compare to the magnificent feline hunters of the past.

Then again, here is Sabine, small member of the family Felidae, order Carnivora. Watch her call upon her greater relatives to track and trap an unsuspecting rat. See her pounce upon the swift salamander. Stand in awe at her predatory prowess.

She has learned how to slip in and out of the Underneath, just as her mother used to do, and she has taught herself to be quick about it. Little Sabine, she is the descendant of the sabertooth, this small silver cat.

But despite her proficiency on the hunt, there were needs she couldn't meet by hunting. She still needed her mother, needed to rest her head on her mother's soft belly, needed to feel her mother's tongue licking her face and ears and chin. And she needed her brother, too. Needed someone to curl up with beneath the tent of Ranger's ear. Needed Puck. And as much as anything, she needed to hear Ranger's song, his deep bluesy voice in the night air. She needed to break the rusted chain that tied Ranger to the post so that the two of them could leave this tilting house, leave the terrible man, leave and never look back.

See Sabine: intrepid hunter.

See Sabine: loyal friend.

See Sabine: lion-hearted.

# 72

WHAT DOES A snake live on when she is trapped in a jar for a thousand years? Even an enchanted being like Grandmother Moccasin needs something to sustain her. Wishes are not enough, surely. A snake cannot survive on those alone, even one with magic in her blood. Grandmother twirled around in her clay prison. Hope filled the jar.

After Night Song slipped into the creek on that night a thousand years ago, Hawk Man went wild with hope. He clung to it like a spider to a web. He was desperate with it. Hope that he was mistaken, that he had misread the terrible tracks in the sand. Hope, bright and slippery, wrapped itself around him.

His daughter, the little girl who glimmered, watched him walk back and forth along the banks of the creek, his feet pounding the red shore, hope urging him on. She listened as he called Night Song's name, called it over and over, until his throat was raw and sore, called some more, hoped that she would swim back to him. Night Song. Hope was caught in his chest, in his legs, his thighs, his feet. He was covered with it, it settled on his skin like sweat. He was so consumed by it that he could not turn his face away from the water. Finally, he stopped pacing and slumped down on the ground beside it.

The girl was afraid that she would lose Hawk Man, too, that he would also disappear. Since she had pointed out her mother's footprints, her father had not even looked at her. All that hope took him away from her, like the night had taken her mother.

When at last Hawk Man stopped his frantic pacing and sat down, the girl walked to his place by the creek and sat next to him. She didn't know what words to say. Didn't have the language for all this loss. So she leaned her head on his shoulder, and then, like she had done when she was just a day old, she held her hand up to him and touched him on the chin. It was the only thing she knew to do.

And finally, for at least a little while, the circling birds settled back into their nests. They had done all they could. As the little girl leaned against Hawk Man, she looked at the jar with its crescent moons and the etching of the huge snake on its surface. She noticed the graceful curves of the serpent's lines, the exactness of the diamond-shaped scales, the large head with its eyes set wide apart. Grandmother. The girl squinted, and when she did, the snake's tongue seemed to flicker, as though it were trying to tell her something. At once the girl knew that here was someone who could tell her what had happened to her mother, one who could explain why her mother had disappeared, one who knew the forest best.

Hope, brilliant, flew onto her shoulders, its invisible feathers ablaze. Hope stirred the air around her, chirred into her ears, whispered the name she needed to say out loud. "Grandmother."

The girl knew what she had to do. She had to find Grandmother Moccasin. Grandmother would know how to help. She would know where to find her mother. She would know how to help her father.

Grandmother, with her old magic. She would know.

# 73

THAT NIGHT, WHILE her father slept, the girl sat up from her mat. Beside her sat the jar. By the tiny fragment of light from the new moon, she rubbed her thumb over the smooth edge of the rim. As she did, she felt the last touches of her mother's own fingers where they had rubbed the smooth surface. The jar seemed to hum. She rose and lifted it into her arms and held on to it as hard as she could. It did not seem as heavy as it had before. Silently she walked out of the hut, and down to the edge of the creek, careful not to wake anyone, especially her hope-filled father.

Once there, she set the jar down again in the soft sand, just as she had done earlier that morning. "I'll return to you," she said, and ran her hand along the smooth curve of its round body. As if in reply, the small crescent moons carved by her mother's thumbnail glinted in the light of the pale moon, tiny sparks in the darkness. Then she turned, put her own feet into her mother's disappearing footsteps, and stepped into the water. It was cold, and she had to gulp to keep from crying out.

As the water came up to her chin, she held her breath and

rolled onto her back. How many times had she floated on the creek's surface? Her mother had taught her how to ride on the back of the current and let the water hold her up. It was just that her mother had always been there with her, holding her as she drifted by, and then pushed her back to the edge of the village. Now here she was, alone in the water. The current that curled around her small body felt swifter than she remembered. She looked over her shoulder and caught a last glimpse of the jar. The etching of Grandmother glowed.

Water splashed over her face. For a moment she felt a small jolt of panic race through her chest, and she began to flail against the push of the water. Then she remembered, Grandmother could tell her what had happened to her mother. She would find Grandmother Moccasin. She relaxed and let the current carry her, carry her along on its steady roll to the south, let her float on its silvery surface until it pushed her to the other side, where she climbed onto the quiet bank and stepped into the deep, deep woods.

Only the trees took notice, and they could not say a thing. If they could have, they would have told the girl that she had gone too far. A thousand years ago this girl in search of Grandmother Moccasin, this one and only daughter of Hawk Man and Night Song, rode the creek to the other side, but she rode too far. Here, then, is a little girl, radiant with hope. Lost.

# 74

SOMEONE ELSE WAS on the hunt. Gar Face. His nights and days were filled with the prospect of trapping and killing the Alligator King. Each night he spent more and more time poling his pirogue along the waters of the large bayou. Several times, the beast had released bubbles underneath his boat. But each time, it was in a different part of the bayou. And it didn't happen every night.

Gar Face knew he was there. He knew that the monster was teasing him. This was no ordinary alligator. He began to consider what it would take to bring the creature in: something for bait, a sturdy chain, a long-handled knife, and his rifle. He clutched his father's rifle in his hand and stared at the murky water.

Determination, brilliant and cold, curled around his heart.

He closed his eyes and envisioned the other trappers and poachers, the ones who sneered at him whenever he drove to the old tavern along the hidden road, that invisible tavern, tucked away beneath the canopy of trees, the blackjacks and junipers, the sweet gums and tupelos. In all the nights he had been there, no one had ever invited him to drink with them, inquired about his health, or asked him what his real name was. He had felt their disgust in the crevices of his broken face. Disgust burrowed deeply into the scars left there by his father.

What would they say when he showed them the skin of a gator a hundred feet long? What name would they give him then?

In her jar Grandmother remembered all her names. *Lamia*, her original and oldest. *Wife*, given to her by her beloved, the one who turned his back on her. *Sister*, bestowed upon her by her reptile cousins, the copperheads, the eastern hognoses, the yellow corn snakes, and also by her friend the Alligator King. *Grandmother Moccasin*, her best known, a tribute from the tribe of cottonmouths. The one that mattered most: *Mother*. That's what Night Song had called her. She tucked her head beneath her scaly body and sighed. *Mother*.

# 75

AFTER SO MANY hours of looking for Night Song, after so much calling and calling, until his throat was raw, after searching in the woods, Hawk Man knew the truth. He did not have to see her to know that Night Song had broken the rule, she had slipped into her serpent skin and was lost to him now. He knew that was the only reason that she had not come home.

Hadn't she known the rule?

He searched his memory, but he could not recall discussing it with her. He had taken it for granted that she had known, just as all the shape-shifters knew. Didn't they? Surely, he thought, her mother had told her. Grandmother Moccasin. She should have told her.

As he tumbled onto his sleeping mat inside his hut, every bone, every muscle, every inch of him exhausted, he fell into a deep, deep sleep. He did not notice the rising of the slim moon. He did not hear his daughter pick up her jar and slip out of the hut. He did not feel the sun rising above the roof and warming the day. Instead, he felt only weariness, thick and hard. He slept and slept and slept.

He slept so long that he got lost in the solitary act of sleeping. And while he slept, he dreamed. He dreamed of stretching his wings and floating on the warm air currents, of soaring over the tops of the trees and looking over the wide and green expanse beneath him. He felt the rush of the breeze as it lifted him, as it curled around him in the sky. He saw the bluey blue of the water far to the south and the inky black of the night as he spun below the stars.

Flight. How long had it been since he had lifted his body up into the sky? More than ten years! Long years. Flight. He missed it, ached for it, longed to spread his arms and soar. Flight.

In his dreams he sailed into the air. Why, he wondered, had he given it all up? He circled the green woods below. Why?

And then he remembered the lullaby, the beautiful song without lyrics, the one that had called directly to him. Night Song! Suddenly flight didn't matter. The only thing that mattered was Night Song. That was all. In his dreams he started falling, spinning, faster and faster. Yes, he had given up his wings for a different kind of flight, the flight of his heart. Night Song.

But there was another, wasn't there?

Another. One who glimmered, whose skin changed colors in the light, his daughter. Yes. His daughter.

He remembered her. He had sung his own song to her, a father's song. Then sleep wrapped its heavy arm around him.

He had another name too: *Father.*

# 76

FROM THE DEEPEST part of the Bayou Tartine, the Alligator King watched each night as the man poled his boat around and around. It was becoming a game to him. He knew that the man was looking for him. He also knew that the man would eventually try to trick him. It was a dangerous game this man was playing.

The Alligator King, however, didn't mind danger. It had been a long time since anyone had tried to hunt him down. Many centuries earlier, a group of them from the old village had ventured into his territory, looking for him.

Alas, they had made the sad mistake of trying to cross the quicksand on the triangle of land between the two bayous. The alligator had pulled himself onto the bank and watched as they slipped beneath the shifting mud. He could still remember their pitiful cries. But he could do nothing to help them, even though he was sorry that the quicksand took them before he could have them for dinner. Alas.

He knew the man in the boat would not make the same mistake. But he also knew that a mistake would be made.

□ □ □

Mistakes. In her underground prison, Grandmother swirled in a circle. Mistakes. *Sssssssstttttt!!!!*

Everyone made mistakes.

And there was always a price to pay.

# 77

AT THE BASE of the old tree, Puck sat just in front of the opening to his den. In these past several days he had accomplished three important things: finding a place to sleep, filling up his belly, and recognizing the moon. But despite these small victories, he couldn't shake the mistake he had made when he broke the rule about the Underneath. Mistake was all around him, right here in his mud-caked fur, here in this patch of sunlight, here in the trees looming overhead. Mistake, mistake, mistake.

Mostly it was in the rushing sound of the salty creek, the last place he had seen his mother. *Promise you'll go back.* It was as if the creek itself were speaking to him. He had promised. He had.

And that promise bound him as tightly as the chain that bound Ranger to the post beside the tilting house.

Ranger. Puck cocked his ears. Why didn't the old hound bay? Without a beacon, Puck had no way of knowing which direction to go. He looked below at the tumbling creek. He blinked. There was the hummingbird. She was there, just over the water, a small rainbow, and then she was gone.

While he watched, a shadow filled up the sunny patch in front of him. He looked up. The bird! It was the same large bird that had dropped the mouse. Puck fluffed up his fur. Was the bird returning for his lost mouse? The little cat hissed. He had scared the bird before, and he could do it again.

But just in case, he slipped into his quiet den and curled up into a circle, a circle of fur and mud and something else.

Loneliness.

As deep as the creek.

# 78

WITH THEIR ROOTS exposed to the very innards of the Earth, where they can feel all its tremors and movements, trees, with their branches skimming the sky, branches that serve as antennae, can tell when something is awry. They knew then, a thousand years earlier, that when Night Song donned her serpent skin she began to die.

From the moment Grandmother told Night Song that she could not return to the village of humans, that she was destined to wear her serpent skin for the rest of her life, the smaller snake had climbed into the branches of the cypress above the bayou and refused to come down. She refused to eat. She also refused to sing.

At first Grandmother left her alone. *Soon she'll feel better*, she thought. Grandmother waited. Grandmother watched.

Then one morning, as the sun began to rise, she looked up to see Night Song and gasped. Her daughter was a different color. Her shiny skin, black as coal, once so black it looked blue, had changed. No longer shiny at all, even in the goldy sun, it looked purplish, with a slight tinge of yellow.

If Night Song were a human, her body might look like a bruise, that color that is the result of blood pooling just beneath the skin. Grandmother was alarmed. She called to Night Song.

*Come to me, my lovely daughter.*

But Night Song could not hear her. The only things she could hear inside her head were the echoing voices of her husband and daughter. Even though neither of them was nearby, that was all she could hear. That was all she would ever hear.

She did not hear Grandmother calling to her.

*Sing, my daughter, sing!*

Did not hear her at all.

Despite Grandmother's desperate pleas for Night Song to eat and swim and sing, the smaller snake remained coiled in the branch, listening only to the two voices she loved so well, listening to them over and over, swirling through her brain, through every diamond scale.

How long did Night Song stay there, losing her color, and listening only to two invisible voices? If you could translate the language of mulberry and tallow and cedar, the trees might tell you that she did not last for very long.

Her colors diminished, the purple turned to lavender, the yellow turned to gray, until finally the morning came when there was no color at all, only the merest shadow of a hollow body. Here was one of the waterfolk dying of heartbreak, becoming transparent, her scales as clear as glass.

And while her diamond scales, one by one, vanished, her own daughter became thoroughly and profoundly lost, far away in a distant part of the forest, all alone, and back in the village her husband was caught in a sleep so deep, he couldn't move.

At last, bereft of all substance, Night Song, beloved by the denizens of the deep, piney woods, and most of all by her husband and daughter, faded into air.

## 79

WHEN THE DAUGHTER of Night Song and Hawk Man stepped out of the creek, she did not realize that she had floated far to the south, much farther than she should have. She shook herself off and leaned against a friendly tupelo tree, waited for the morning to drift through the branches and offer her some light.

She looked around. Nothing was familiar. She blinked her eyes to try to get her bearings, to try to remember what her mother had told her about finding Grandmother.

*Cross the creek to the other side and walk until you get to a place where the ground is so soft, your footsteps will fill with water. Go, and go some more. When you find the place where the cypress trees grow in the middle of the water, where the moss drapes down like curtains, so thick they shade the sun, where the land shifts and sways, there you'll find Grandmother.*

She stared at the landscape in front of her. To an unknowing eye, it might look just the same as the landscape that surrounded her village. But when a girl grows up in a thick forest, she knows the trees, knows their differences and similarities. The trees she saw here were not unusual. But there were too many spaces in between. Here, the pines and hollies and winged elms were not as close to one another, their branches did not intertwine as tightly as those pines and hollies and winged elms that she knew, they were more spread out, the gaps between their trunks were wider. She looked up and realized that she could see more of the sky than she ever had, open and blue. So much sky, so much blue. She stretched her arms and let it settle on her skin. For a small moment she felt happy.

But then she looked at her feet and realized that the ground here was different too. There was more grass and fewer pine needles. It was firmer than the soft ground of the wetlands that she knew so well. She looked around. Where was she?

This could not be the way to the deep cypress groves. This could not be the dark area where the bayous met. The ground was too hard, the trees were too sparse. The sky was too big.

"Where am I?" she asked.

## 80

A THOUSAND YEARS later, a small gray cat with a patch of silver fur looked out across the creek and asked the same question. Below, the water tumbled by, whispering as it rolled. *Here and here and here*, it seemed to chant. Puck wondered. Where was here? Where was Sabine, his twin? Where was Ranger, his hound-dog papa? Where was his home in the Underneath?

He considered the answering creek. *Here and here and here*, it whispered back. The creek was taunting him. He looked to the other side. He had to get across. Somehow. Some way. Soon.

# 81

WHEN NIGHT SONG vanished, Grandmother did not weep at all. Instead, she was furious that her daughter had left her once more. She became ravenous. She swallowed anything that moved. She could not be satisfied. Instead of sleeping, she caught mice and rats and foxes. Instead of napping, she dove into the bayou and swallowed up fish and baby alligators and anything else that swam—mink, beaver, even other snakes.

Her scissor-like jaws grabbed onto their bodies and snapped them like twigs. Anything unfortunate enough to cross her path was likely to be sliced in two. Do not look into that mouth of cotton. That terrible cotton mouth.

Her appetite was enormous, and so was she. She grew and grew and grew. And as she grew, so too did her anger. Her daughter had chosen another over her. Two anothers.

Hawk Man.

The daughter.

Hawk Man.

The daughter.

Hawk Man.

And then . . . *Ahh*, thought Grandmother. *The daughter.* At last she paused in her ravenous binging. *The daughter.* And she remembered the glimmering girl. Night Song's daughter.

In the next breath, she said, *If I cannot have Night Song, I'll take the daughter.*

And she began to laugh, a high-pitched, careening laugh, a laugh that made the trees shiver. *Yes*, she thought, *I'll take the daughter.* She curled up on the stump of the old cypress and began to make a plan.

She would bring the child to her dark lair and keep her there. She would teach her the ways of the creeks and bayous, show her the underwater caves of the crawdads, introduce her to her alligator cousin. Together they would turn their backs on the humans. Imagining it made her smile. Soon the daughter would adore her, just as Night Song once had. No longer would she be alone with only her vengeance as company. *Sssooooon*, she hissed, *ssssooooon my time will come.*

And this time she would not be so naive. She would be more watchful, more fastidious in her keep. Once a creature has been adored, she never forgets it. Grandmother had not forgotten Night Song's adoration. But this time she would not take the adoration for granted. She would not let this one go.

The Alligator King, hearing of her plan, asked, "Sister, what if the child cannot step out of her human skin?"

Grandmother paused. This was something she had not considered. It caused her momentary consternation. But then she smiled.

"This child is shot through with old magic," she said. "A human shape is not her only one."

"How can you be sure?" asked the alligator.

"She's the daughter of Night Song, is she not?"

The alligator blinked his yellow eyes. "No matter what her shape, a child is a child."

Grandmother hissed, "She's mine." Then she added, "I'll take the daughter."

And with that, she stretched her long body and began her crawl back toward the Caddo village. She did not know that the child was looking for her, too. She did not know that the child was lost.

Grandmother slithered over the pine needle floor, slipped in and out of the marshes, skimmed over the boggy fens.

*Daughter. I'll take the daughter.* She chanted it over and over as she crawled toward the creek, toward the village of the humans, toward the girl who glimmered. *Sssssstttt. I'll take her for my own.*

At last the edge of the creek came up to greet her. She skimmed along the shallows, cool around her huge body. She raised her head. Where was the girl? The daughter? She should be near here, shouldn't she? Shouldn't she be drawn to the water, like her ancient forebears?

She looked over the side of the bank. All she saw was a jar, gleaming in the afternoon sun.

## 82

WHILE HAWK MAN slept, the birds kept vigil outside his hut, the falcons and sparrows and blue jays, the catbirds and cardinals and painted buntings. They called to him.

*Brother! Step out of your human skin.*

He sank ever deeper into sleep. There was a rule. A rule he was bound by. That old rule: Once you forsake your human skin, you can never go back. He had known this. Why hadn't Night Song?

*Don your feathers*, cried the birds, the spotted owls and nighthawks, the whip-poor-wills and bobwhites.

*Fly away with us*, called the killdeer and mockingbirds and the black-bellied plovers.

But he couldn't. He had a daughter. What about his daughter? She was a human. He had to keep his human shape for her. If he took back his feathered body, he would be lost to her, just as Night Song was lost to both of them. Weariness coursed through his body, drugged him into more sleep.

Sleep. All-consuming sleep pulled him into a huge, quiet emptiness. And all the while the birds, the red-winged blackbirds, the tiny finches, the mourning doves, circled in the air above.

After three long days and nights, he finally woke up. His dark eyes with glints of gold were crusted from the tears that had fallen while he slept. He brushed them with his fingers. He looked around the room. Empty. Such emptiness. A huge and overwhelming emptiness.

The mat beside him where Night Song had slept was still empty. He rubbed his hand over it. Then he looked at the other side of the hut. The mat where his daughter slept was empty too.

His daughter! Where was she? How long had he been asleep? How long had she been gone? And then he noticed. The jar was gone too.

## 83

CATS ARE BUILT for naps, and Puck was no exception. He spent a lot of time snoozing. In between, he worked on his hunting skills until soon he became adept at sneaking up on the tiny mice that built their nests just beneath the long red needles of the towering pines. He added an occasional salamander and tree frog, although this latter was more fun to catch than to eat.

Hunting made him think of his sister. Sabine. He remembered how she lay in wait for him beside the old fish traps, then leapt out at him, front paws raised above her head, all spit and fur. *Hiisssss!!!* It made him smile.

With his belly full of a juicy mouse, he thought she might be just a little proud of him. He sat on the edge of the salty creek and looked down at the water. When he closed his eyes, he could almost feel his mother right beside him, licking the mud off his tattered gray coat. For the first time in many days, he purred.

Purring is not so different from praying. To a tree, a cat's purr is one of the purest of all prayers, for in it lies a whole mixture of gratitude and longing, the twin ingredients of every prayer. Here then is a small cat, purring, praying that he will find his way to his sister and Ranger. He opened his eyes and looked to the other side of the creek. They were out there, somewhere.

*Promise*, his mother had said. And he had.

Promise smoldered inside him, like an ember. But unlike that warm desire, the creek was cold and deep. And now it had become something else. An enemy. And like any other enemy, this one was clever and crafty. It taunted him and hissed at him as it rolled down to the river. Puck was sure that it could swallow him, just as it had swallowed his mother.

So he watched.

And watched.

Then, one day, on the surface of the water, he saw a large limb floating along. The limb bumped from one side of the creek to the other.

He might have ignored it. He had seen many limbs do the same thing. But on this particularly sunny day, on this particularly large limb, he noticed five sawback turtles riding atop the limb. There they sat, perched like birds on a branch. Just like that.

Yes, that's right. They were riding the limb. On top of the water.

Puck sat up. He watched the turtles. Now they were on this side of the creek. Next they bumped against the other side of the creek. *The other side.* Where he wanted to go. Over there. Turtles on a limb.

Then he realized that if he ran downstream just a short way, he could meet the tacking limb and jump aboard. Then it would carry him to the other side, just like it carried the turtles. The simplicity of it took his breath away. Yes, he would ride the limb to the other side and jump off. If turtles could do it, so could he.

He jumped up and started following the floating turtle boat. At first he trotted beside it, keeping it parallel to him on the bank, but quickly he saw that he needed to get ahead of it so that it would come to him. He picked up his pace and ran. Finally he came to a small bend and looked over his shoulder. He could see the limb heading straight toward him.

Closer and closer and closer. *Almost.*

Yes!

He slid down the bank and landed, *oomph*, right in front of the turtle-laden limb.

He closed his eyes and . . .

jumped!

As soon as he leapt onto the log, the startled turtles slid into the water. That combination, leaping cat/sliding turtles, set the limb to spinning. Puck ran, the limb spun. Puck was a swift cat. He could run fairly fast, but not fast enough to outrun the spinning limb. Soon he dug in his claws, all of them, as hard as he could, which turned out to be a bigger mistake, because it just meant that he was stuck to the limb when he went under.

*Splash!*

The cold of the water shocked him. He gulped in a large mouthful and started choking.

*Meow!!!*

Fortunately, all that spinning had kept the limb right beside the shore. So even though he had taken a good dunking, once he righted himself, he was only up to his belly in water. He coughed the last of the water up. Then he climbed onto the bank and caught his breath. When he looked up, the turtles were climbing back aboard and floating away. They didn't even look back at him. He sat down and watched. Then he looked again at the opposite shore. It seemed farther away than ever.

He licked his wet coat and coughed.

The only good thing that had come of his experiment in sailing was this: The cold water had loosened the last of the old mud, and his coat, though completely wet, was now completely clean.

This was small consolation. A clean coat did not get him any closer to the other side of the creek. He shook his wet fur, first one paw, then another, then his whole body. He sent the water scattering into the air around him, tiny prisms in the afternoon sun.

As the drops settled, he heard the rapid thrumming of wings just behind him. He looked over his shoulder. There she was again.

The hummingbird.

Here.

There.

Gone.

# 84

GO BACK A thousand years, to this same spot along the creek, here beneath the trees. Go back to the moment when Grandmother slithered along its bank, in search of her granddaughter, the little girl who glimmered.

On that day the sun shone like a spotlight on the abandoned jar. Grandmother looked at it. She had seen it before, only days ago when she had come to fetch Night Song. Seen how the threesome, Night Song, Hawk Man, the daughter, had joined hands around the jar. She had seen them together, seen their embraces, their smiles. Now she pulled her huge body onto the bank and began to slowly circle the jar.

Here was a jar of beauty, graceful in its round and perfect symmetrical shape, large in its size. Here was a jar that was built for utility, for holding water and berries and grain. But here also was a jar for admiring. Grandmother noticed the artistry, the band of crescent moons that ringed the rim.

But ahh . . . the snake etched on the side. That was something to behold. Grandmother lifted her head and ran her chin along its curved lines, traced it with her tongue. She sat back. Night Song!

She could smell her daughter's presence, pressed into the hard clay. She breathed in the wonder of it. This jar. This lovely jar, made by her own daughter. Then she hissed. *Sssssssttttt!!!*

Night Song! If it weren't for Night Song, she wouldn't be so lonely. Night Song had abandoned her, not once, but twice. She drew herself up and prepared to strike the jar. With her terrible jaws, she could crack the rim and destroy it. She curled herself into a coil, felt the poison pool in her mouth, felt the tension build in her million curved bones, her sinewy muscles.

This jar was her enemy. This jar made by Night Song. The jar with her very own image on the outside. She drew back like an arrow on a bow and opened her cotton mouth. . . .

But at the moment of striking, that moment when every muscle was taut and ready, she suddenly felt something grab her from behind, felt a tight grip around her neck like a vise.

She sputtered and spit. She twisted and curved, whipped her body around and around. She gagged. The grip around her neck was tight. Tight. She tasted her own poison as it spewed onto her thin tongue. She felt droplets of moisture seep out of her diamond scales, run down her body. She twisted again. The grip tightened.

"You!" She heard a deep voice. And all at once, she knew who it was. Hawk Man.

He turned her around so that she was facing him. His hand held her at arm's length from his face. Otherwise she would strike him directly on the face. But she could do nothing right now.

He had her in his hand. She could see the glints of gold flashing in his dark eyes. She noticed the feathers growing in his hair. Ahhh, she realized, this was no ordinary man.

He looked directly into her eyes and spoke.

"What have you done with them?" he said.

"Night Song is gone," she answered. Then she added, with a sneer, "She was done with you." She saw the flash of sadness, just a glimmer of it, in his eye. But it wasn't there for long. She told him, "It's too late for Night Song."

She expected him to break down, to weep, as humans do. But instead he started shaking her. "What did you do with my daughter?"

The shaking made her cough. She sputtered and spit. The poison ran down her throat. "What do you mean?" she asked.

"Where is she? What did you do with her?"

In that moment, Grandmother realized, here was a man at her mercy. Here was a man she could use for her own devices. She would lie to him to make him put her down, then she would quickly dispatch him and go on her own hunt for her granddaughter. Yes, the daughter. Soon, she would be all hers.

And this ploy might have worked if she had moved faster, but before she could say anything, Hawk Man squeezed her again, and when he did, her body convulsed and her tail, like a whip, slashed across the skin on Hawk Man's thigh, opening a wide and gaping wound.

Hawk Man howled in pain.

Here was a man in agony, a man who had lost his wife, a man who could not find his little daughter. Hawk Man was done with sorrow and hope and dreams. Here was a man who was furious.

And in his rage, he lifted the lid on his daughter's jar, the large and wonderful jar, and stuffed Grandmother into it, forced her enormous and thrashing body into the deep, smooth jar, a jar meant for carrying fresh water and crawdads, meant for storing corn and grain, meant as a gift from a mother to a daughter.

"Your time has come!" he shouted.

He jammed the old serpent down into the beautiful jar and slammed the tight-fitting lid on top. And just to be certain that the lid would not come free, he lifted a large, heavy stone from the side of the creek and set it on top.

Then he began to dig. With his bare hands, he dug and dug and dug, through the hard and sticky clay beside the creek, until at last he had a deep hole, a hole that was perfect for burying a jar. This jar. With its terrible contents.

As he lowered the jar and covered the hole with dirt, he did not notice the puncture wound. In the pain he felt on his thigh where Grandmother's vicious tail had slashed him, he did not notice the pain in his hand, did not see the swelling that started there and began to race up his arm, did not feel the poison racing through his veins, his arteries, coursing through his own enchanted blood, the blood of the phoenix, the roc, of Thoth himself, the ancient birds of magic, those old and forgotten shifters of shape, those birds.

Something else he did not notice: the pine cone, brushed into the hole, the pine cone that would lay there, just below the surface, through a long and thirsty drought, until at last a furious fire cracked the cone open and beckoned it to sprout, to spread its roots into the red clay beside the creek and encircle the jar in their web, to send its small trunk up toward the sun, where it would widen and reach, widen and reach, where it would stand for a thousand years through thousands of storms, until one storm in its last breath of wind would send out a bolt of lightning that would carve a large and fiery slash deep into its trunk, beckoning the end.

This tree.

This large and lovely tree.

# 85

GAR FACE KNEW that the alligator was toying with him, playing a game. It made him angry. Every night, the same. He waited on the water's edge for the bubbles to appear. Then he steered his boat toward them, only to arrive and see the bubbles rise up behind him.

He took a deep draught from his flask. Vodka. It was cheap and wicked, and it burned going down. There it settled in his gut, burning even more.

The alligator, mixed with the alcohol, was making Gar Face simmer from the inside out. Then one night, as he pushed his boat toward the bank, he heard a bump on the bottom of the pirogue. Many times his boat had been bumped by alligators or fish, or even the rat-like nutria that had moved here during the last century. Water rats, they feasted on the lilies that grew along the shore and built their dens out of mud.

*Bump!* There it was again.

*Bump, bump, bump!* Again and again and again.

Gar Face knew. This was not a water rat or a fish. The boat began to rock from side to side. Gar Face sat down, hard. The pole that he used for steering slipped into the water. With a sensation of horror, he realized he was stranded. The shore was only a yard away, close enough to step outside the boat and pull it to the banks.

But he knew that if he put a foot over the edge, the alligator would take him down. All at once, Gar Face was furious! He swore at the beast beneath him, even as the boat rocked and rocked. He felt the vodka rise in his throat, tasted the bitterness of his own bile.

*Bump, bump, bump!*

Rock, rock, rock.

The boat began to spin in a circle as if it were trapped in a whirlpool.

"SSSTTOOOPPP!!!!!"

As soon as the hoarse yell escaped his throat, the bumping ceased, but the boat continued to spin. Dizziness engulfed him. The yell that had split the air seemed to sink into the bayou along with the alligator. Gar Face lifted his flask to his mouth and drank, long and hard.

The liquid slid down his throat like a salve. The boat rocked again, this time gently, atop the water. It had been a long time, twenty-five years to be exact, since the night he had chased the deer to its death in the woods, a quarter century since he had felt so close to panic. An unpleasant tick of fear crawled across his chest. He panted.

Then he sneered. He had won then. He would win now. He

raised his flask to the beast in the water and saluted. Then he took another deep draft. His insides burned.

When he looked over the edge of the boat, he saw that it was pushed up against the shore. He did not remember feeling the boat move in this direction. He took another hard swallow of the wicked vodka. Then he stood up, his legs shaking, and quickly jumped onto the grass and pulled the boat up with him. His head swam. He felt the bile mixed with vodka in his stomach begin to rise in his throat, and it made him nauseous; he sank onto the ground. He closed his eyes to steady himself, but it didn't help. Instead he lay down in the marshy grass. The last thing he heard was the high-pitched whine of the early-morning mosquitoes, settling in for breakfast.

## 86

AT THE TILTING house, Sabine knew that something was wrong. The morning sun was well into the sky and the man had not returned. This was unusual. For her entire life, the man had left the house just as the sun had settled beyond the trees, and returned just as it rose.

She relied on Gar Face's regular schedule to do her evening hunting. She knew that as soon as the man left, she could slip out from the Underneath, find something to eat, and return before he came back. She had been back now for hours. And the man was still gone.

Sabine would have loved nothing more than for the man to never come back. Then she could be free of the fear she harbored of him. There was just one problem. Ranger's chain. They still needed the man to feed Ranger, even if he sometimes forgot.

With Ranger tied to the chain, he could not join her on the hunt. She compensated by bringing home small lizards and mice for him. He was always grateful, but they were never enough.

What would happen if the man never returned and Ranger remained chained to the post?

*No*, she thought, *surely he'll return*. She turned toward the dark corner where Ranger lay, asleep, and rubbed against her old friend, tucked herself under his big ear and started to purr. Ranger stirred. His stomach was empty and he was thirsty, too. But Sabine was curled next to him, her soft purrs filling his head.

Little Sabine. She was the only one left for him. Faithful Sabine. How could he ever tell her how much he loved her, how much she meant to him?

He tried to go back to sleep, but he, too, worried about Gar Face's absence. As much as he hated his owner, he needed him for food and water. Surely he, Ranger, didn't deserve to die by starving at the end of a chain. Surely.

# 87

PUCK LOST TRACK of how much time had passed since he had pulled himself out of the creek. All he knew was that with each day, his urge to cross it grew stronger. Each day his mother's voice echoed in his ears. *Promise. Promise you'll go back.*

And each morning, after he had eaten, he walked to the bank and looked down at his nemesis, the creek. On the other side, he knew, were his sister and the hound. But even if he could get across, how would he find them? Which way would he go? He needed a beacon, a signal, some way to locate the right direction.

Why didn't Ranger bay? How many times had he asked this question, over and over and over? And how many times had he left it there, unanswered? But today, standing on the edge of the creek, the awful answer presented itself, an answer he had avoided all this time.

Q: Why didn't Ranger bay?

A: Something awful must have happened.

There it was, right in front of him, where it had been all this time, lurking like a shadow. *Hhhiiiissssss!* The truth of it buzzed in his ears. The fur on his back stood up.

Something awful must have happened.

The certainty of it was like a gust of wind, knocking against his bones. That was the only answer, Puck knew it. If it weren't so, Ranger surely would have howled by now, he would have held his head up and bayed for his small gray kitten and for the mama cat, too.

Something awful must have happened.

The sun grew higher in the sky. The creek boiled as it tumbled by. Puck had to get back to the tilting house. Something awful must have happened. He was about to hiss again, when . . .

*Chat-chat-chat-chat-chat.*

The sudden noise startled him. He looked around but couldn't see anything.

*Chat-chat-chat-chat-chat.*

Puck spun in a circle. No one was near. He looked in the spots of sunlight on the forest floor all around him, but there were no bird shadows flying through them.

*Chat-chat-chat-chat.*

Where was it coming from? Then a shower of acorn husks fell down from the oak tree that stood near his den. He looked up.

*Chat-chat-chat-chat-chat.*

A squirrel! Puck could barely detect the sleek brown animal, it was so far up in the branches of the tree. It was the tail that gave it away. From where he stood, he could see the brushy tail swishing to and fro.

He had never seen any animal besides a bird so high up in a

tree before. How high up was it? Twenty feet? Thirty? The height impressed him. Then, in a flash, the squirrel zipped from one limb to another, walked out to the very ends of the smallest branches and ran along their narrow limbs. He stopped only long enough to shell an acorn and drop the husk on the ground.

Puck continued to watch. The squirrel scurried from one tree to another tree, from one branch to another branch, from one thin limb to another thin limb, until he did the impossible, and made it look easy: The squirrel crossed the creek.

Puck sat down hard, his mouth agape in wonder.

On the other side, the small animal disappeared in the thick brush. Why hadn't Puck thought of that? He looked at his sharp claws. Didn't he have the equipment for climbing trees? He growled a little and scratched the air. He sat up straight and licked his right shoulder.

He looked after the now vanished squirrel. He looked into the branches of the trees. He looked to the other side of the creek. There, there on the other side, was where he needed to be.

Grandmother knew where she needed to be too: anywhere but this jar, the birthday jar. A thousand birthdays had gone by, a thousand years in her solitary chamber. She opened her cotton white mouth and yawned. *Ssssoooooonnnn*, she hissed, *my time will come.*

# 88

IT WAS MIDDAY when Gar Face finally awoke. The sun was burning its way through the treetops and eating away at his cheeks. He blinked. It had been years since he had been outside in the full daylight. He wasn't used to it, and his eyes ached when he opened them.

He rubbed his face. It was on fire! His hands, too. He looked at the backs of them. They were covered in lumps and bumps. All morning long, since he had passed out on the bank of the Bayou Tartine, mosquitoes had made a feast of his hands and face. And then the blazing sun had baked his sallow skin to a bright, ugly red. He pulled himself up and walked to the water's edge. He dipped his hands into the coolness of it and splashed his face.

The water smelled old, as if it had sat in this fetid bayou for a million years, and it had. This old bayou, this Bayou Tartine. At the bottom sat the Alligator King, sound asleep.

Gar Face winced at his burning face. Then he drew himself up and walked through the forest, along a path that only he knew to walk, a path that skimmed the edges of the shifting sands. He walked toward the tilting house. He listened for the dog to howl, but he didn't hear it. Stupid dog. What good was a hound that didn't howl?

As he entered the litter-strewn yard, from the corner of his eye he saw something slip beneath the porch. *Fool dog can't even keep rats out of the yard*, he thought. He stepped onto the porch and rested his rifle on the railing. He tugged on the chain to see if the old dog was still alive. Sure enough, Ranger dragged himself out and sat down; he licked his sore leg, the one that still bore the bullet. Gar Face looked at him. The hound looked the same way he felt—tattered and scarred. He reached into the bag that sat on the porch and threw a few nuggets of cheap dog food into the hound's bowl.

Then he walked inside and fell onto his cot. But just before he drifted off, he realized: the animal, the one that had slipped underneath the porch, that was no rat. That was a cat. *Ahh*, he thought.

*Bait.*

# 89

THE PINEY WOODS is home to an abundance of trappers, including the carnivorous pitcher plants whose inviting throats are lined with a sweet, sticky syrup for catching damselflies and other bugs. Spiders, of course, are the royalty of the trapping set with their treacherous webs.

Ask a tree, and it will tell you about any number of traps. The steel traps of hunters, the steel jaws of gators, the vicious jaws of the water moccasins.

From the Underneath, Sabine watched. At last she could rest. The man had returned, and he had actually fed Ranger. She tucked her feet beneath her and closed her eyes. How could she know that a trap was being set?

A tree's memory is long, very long. So is Grandmother Moccasin's. But her memory of the outside world only went up to the moment she was trapped in the jar. She had no recollection of the events that transpired while she lay entombed in her underground chamber. How could she?

# 90

THERE ARE MANY things Grandmother doesn't know, alone in her underground prison. She doesn't know what happened to Hawk Man.

Spent from his struggle with Grandmother Moccasin, he was racked with pain from the wound in his leg where Grandmother's tail had slashed the skin, burning from the venom running through his body, the thick and awful poison that coursed through his veins.

There was all of that. Any other man might lie atop the water of the creek and let it carry him, broken, all the way to the great river to the south, the wide and silver Sabine, and then down to the warm and welcoming Gulf of Mexico, carry him down down down to the bottom of the deep blue sea.

But Hawk Man was no ordinary man. No. His blood was the blood of the great birds of enchantment, of Garuda and Thoth, the old bird gods of India and Egypt, full of the ancient magic. So he waited, waited in pain with his open wound and the toxic poison, each breath an agony, each movement an ache that shot through his entire body. He waited and waited for his daughter to return, his body too sick to go after her. He kept his human form because he, unlike Night Song, knew that once he donned his avian shape he could never return as a human.

He would stay in his human skin for his daughter. So he waited beside the creek, this creek. And while he waited, the villagers brought food to him, bowls of corn and berries and cooked rabbit and even roasted bison. They sat beside him and sang to him. The gentle and loving Caddo, those people who had welcomed him and his family into their tribe. They watched him. They waited with him.

Here, beside this creek, this old and rambling creek.

But they were not the only ones. The birds, too, the peregrines and robins, the jackdaws and vireos. They perched in the branches all around. They circled the sky above him. They nestled in the trees closest to him. They knew that if he stayed in his human skin, the poison would soon kill him.

*Brother! Don your feathers, fly away.*

Each day he grew weaker, but he refused to listen to their calls.

*Step out of your human skin. Fly, brother, fly!*

What about his daughter? Where was she? He began to cough and choke. The poison was filling up his lungs, his chest, his throat.

*Come with us!* cried the blue jays, the wrens, the kinglets, the bobolinks.

*Fly!* called the wood ducks, the cranes, the great blue herons.

He turned his back. He closed his eyes. His daughter. He had to wait for her. He gasped for air. His leg throbbed. The pain racked every inch of him. "My daughter," he cried.

And then, in the fading light, he heard a whirring sound, a soft chirring, the beating of tiny wings. "Come," he heard, "your time has come." He looked up, and there in the golden sunlight was the hummingbird. He smiled, and when he did, she brushed his chin with her wing.

When the villagers came to him next, bearing food and friendship, in the place where their brother had lain for so many days, along the side of the creek, all they found were feathers, feathers that shone copper in the bright rays of the sun. And this is how the creek earned its name, Full of Sorrow for the Little Girl. And over time, that long name was changed until it became the one it is now, still full of tears, the Little Sorrowful, running toward the sea.

# 91

AND WHAT BECAME of the daughter, the one who glimmered? According to the reports of trees, of acacias and birches and tallows, the daughter of Hawk Man and Night Song was lost. For days she had walked, but the ground got harder and the trees more sparse. She had grown up with the sun in patches, filtered through the thick branches of the nannyberries, the water oaks, the maples. Now there was too much sun, and it burned her glimmering skin. The sky she knew was a sky that was broken into pieces, small snatches that peeked between the needles of the tall and whispering pines, but here, in this open place, the sky was enormous and empty.

Beneath her, the ground was solid, and tall grasses surrounded her, bent and bowed in the wind. The forest had always protected her from wind. Here, she was buffeted by it, surrounded by it. Here in this grassy meadow. This meadow full of air.

The air. Ahh, the air. She had never felt so much air surround her at one time. Such softness. Such tenderness. All this air.

Some say that a grassy meadow resembles the sea, that the grass rolls in the wind the way that water rolls into waves. They say that if you close your eyes, you can feel the Earth rock to and fro, back and forth, as though you were on a boat.

For a small girl all by herself, it didn't matter whether she was lost at sea or lost in a meadow. A lost girl is lonely, lonely without her mother, a mother who sang to her every night, lonely without her father, lost in his torments. A girl who has gone to look for her grandmother, a grandmother she has never met. This girl. This mistaken girl. This small glimmering girl all alone in a faraway meadow.

She looked at the blowy grass and the bright blue sky. The enormity of her situation settled on her like a mist. She looked at the world all around, and all at once she knew that she would never see her mother again.

How did she know this? How do any of us know these things? It could be that somehow, if we stand still long enough, we can actually hear the trees and understand their messages. It could be that the light from the sun slips down at a certain slant so as to fill us in. Maybe it's just that love has its own way of informing us when loss is at hand.

The daughter of Night Song and Hawk Man knew, and right then she felt so small, so tiny, as though she were the smallest creature on the planet.

Any other girl in this situation might curl up in a tight ball and weep and weep and weep. But not this girl, descendant of the sealfolk, the mermen, the sirens.

The blood of the water folk was not the only enchanted blood that ran through her veins. She was also the child of Hawk Man, son of the bird people. And here in this meadow, surrounded by so much air, enwrapped by so much sky, she lifted her arms toward the clouds. Her skin, radiant in the sun's light, flashed all the colors of the rainbow. Suddenly the sky filled up with birds, a host of swallows and martins and painted buntings, of boat-tailed grackles and red-cockaded woodpeckers, bobwhites and mockingbirds. A million different birds, calling in their million different voices.

*Daughter*, they cried. *Step out of your human skin.*

They dipped and swirled in the air above her, and as they did, brilliant-colored feathers grew in her hair and covered her arms and neck and body, a rainbow of feathers. And all at once, in a flash of light, she flew away, flew so fast it seemed the air swallowed her right up.

Trapped in her jar, Grandmother felt a wave of longing rush through her. Would she ever see the goldy sun? Or her friend the alligator? Would she ever know the feel of wind and rain and the silver moon against her skin? Skin. For a thousand years, the only skin she had touched was her own. Dry and brittle. Skin. She would trade her own skin to hear Night Song's lullaby one more time, to see her granddaughter glimmer in the light of the sun. She slashed her tail against the curve of the jar. Her skin ached.

# 92

IN THE SOLEMN Underneath, Sabine went about her regular routine. She did not know that Gar Face was aware of her, or that he was making plans that included her. Over the next couple of days, he resumed his normal pattern, leaving the house at dusk and returning in the early morning. She did not know that after he had spotted her, he had gone inside the house and wiped a clear space in the dust on the grimy window. There he peered through it long enough to see her slip out from under the house on her daily hunt. Then he looked at Ranger beside his empty food bowl. "Stupid dog," he sneered. "Let the cat feed you."

He rubbed the windowpane with the cuff of his shirt. Then he rubbed his face with his rough fingers. He was eaten up, as they say, from his mosquito bites and sunburn, his skin swollen and sore.

But he was eaten up by more than insect bites and sunburn. The ache in his face and the top of his hands was nothing compared to the gnawing in his gut, the one that ate at him from the inside.

Later he sat on his porch and cleaned his old rifle. The stand-off between himself and the Alligator King had become personal now. No longer would he go out on the water, no. From now on, he'd stay on the land. The water was the true domain of the gator. On the water, the advantage lay with the gator.

Gar Face rubbed the stock of his gun and smirked. "I'll lure him onto the shore, and then ..." He held the gun up to his angry face and looked through the scope.

In the Underneath, Ranger and Sabine sat close together. The bullet in Ranger's front leg burned. But Ranger didn't complain. Instead he licked Sabine on the top of her head and looked across the rancid yard and into the thick woods, where fireflies blinked on and off. The chain around his neck felt heavier than ever.

Just as the sun began to set, he saw something hovering right at the tree line, right there where the trees ran up to the edge of the yard. It was a tiny rainbow, bouncing up and down, to and fro. He blinked. A hummingbird?

He knew what a hummingbird meant. But whom had she come for? He licked his wounded leg. The bullet lodged there cooled down.

On the porch above, Gar Face saw the hummingbird too. He held his rifle against his sunburned cheek and looked through the crosshairs at the end of the barrel. He squeezed the trigger. *BOOM!!!* When he looked up, the bird was gone. He had no way of knowing whether or not he'd shot it. If he had, the bird would have evaporated entirely. There would be no trace left. He didn't care. He wasn't on the hunt for a hummingbird.

Below, Sabine cringed. She had not heard the crack of the rifle for a very long time. To her, the rifle meant that something had died, that a life had been robbed. She remembered the lessons of her mother and Ranger. She knew about the bullet in Ranger's leg. She had seen the skins nailed to the porch railings. *Do not get in front of the man and the rifle. Do not.* It was a good rule.

## 93

PUCK FIGURED OUT that if he imitated the squirrel and ran quickly from limb to limb, he could get across the creek.

He had no trouble getting to the upper story of the tupelo tree. With his sharp claws, he had scampered right up. From his lofty perch, the creek looked very small to Puck now, as though he could simply skip over it. When he looked out, he could see other squirrels jumping from limb to limb, master acrobats. If he looked directly down, he could see the ground.

He should not have looked directly down. Yikes! Down was . . . very . . . far . . . away.

But he was also determined. Looking out from the top of the tree, Puck was more sure than ever that Ranger and Sabine were on the other side. He felt the gentle breeze slipping around him and beneath him. If he stepped out onto it he almost felt like he could fly.

But of course it was not the air that he needed to step onto. It was another branch, and then another and after that, yet another. But every time he moved toward the thin end of the branch in the tupelo, it started to bounce up and down, as though it was trying to buck him off. Each step caused a bounce, which made him back up to his spot near the trunk, where the branch was thick and sturdy. How did the squirrel do it? Race along the skinny branches without making them bounce?

He sat very still for several moments. Then he heard a familiar sound.

*Chat-chat-chat-chat-chat!*

The same squirrel he had seen yesterday was in the tree beside him, twitching his fluffy tail like a flag.

*Chat-chat-chat-chat-chat!*

Puck watched it again as it flitted from one branch to another, from one tree to the next. He paid attention to the way the squirrel scurried to the very end of a thin limb and then leapt across to another. The move was graceful and clean. And *fast*.

*Fast!* That was the key. It must be his *slow* that was making the limb buck up and down. He should go *fast*. Not *slow*.

He watched for a moment longer until the squirrel was once again lost in the foliage. Puck moved toward the end of his own branch, first one paw, then another. He took a deep breath and . . . *fast*.

*Go fast.*

*Go, Puck, go!*

But he only went a few inches. The branch bucked. He dug his claws into the bark. He waited for the branch to stop its up-

and-down motion. Puck's stomach felt queasy. He changed his mind about *fast* and decided to do *slow* again.

He inched along. The branch became thinner and thinner. He paused and looked at the tree next door. There was a waiting limb. It was reaching for him, holding out its leafy fingers. If he just took a running leap he could make it.

He crept to the middle. The branch bounced. Up. Down. He dug in his claws and held on. Then he decided to count down . . . one . . . two . . . three . . .

*BOOM!*

The sound of a rifle split the air.

Puck let go.

# 94

EVEN FROM THE deepest bottom of the bayou, the Alligator King could tell that changes were nigh. Several nights had passed and the boatman had not returned.

*He'll be back*, he thought. *His kind always returns.*

He floated to the top of the water and peered out with his bright yellow eyes. His nostrils broke the surface, and he took a deep breath. "Rain," he said. "It's coming." And with that, he sank back down to the muddy, muddy bottom and fell asleep.

# 95

THE OLD LOBLOLLY pine, the one that stood by the edge of the creek, could also tell that rain was nigh. Now only twenty feet high or so at best, it could feel the storm brewing. Far to the south, the tree knew that this would be a good one.

Trees are always the first to know about storms. This storm, the one on its way from the Gulf of Mexico and up the wide and wandering Sabine, had started off the coast of western Africa, carried the warm winds of the Sahara all the way across the Atlantic Ocean. For a while, it lingered near Cuba and Jamaica before it scuttled over the Gulf. Now it was gathering up the warm waters of the Laguna Madre.

Soon this storm would blow through these piney woods. And it would pack a punch. Batten your hatches. Close your doors. Do not go out into that stormy night.

# 96

THE NIGHT WAS just rising, dark slowly filled in the spaces between the leaves. The stillness of it made Gar Face uneasy. He reached for the flask in his pocket and uncorked it. It was empty, like the dog's food bowl.

Perhaps he could go a whole night without the bitter liquid, perhaps. But why should he? The night was still young. The dog could wait. Besides, why waste food on a dog who was doomed? He shook his head and spit at the ground.

Then he climbed into the old pickup truck resting above a pool of oil. It took several turns of the key to get it going, but at last the engine cranked to a rumbling start. He steered it out of the yard and turned it toward the tavern beside the hidden road.

Tonight, he would listen to them again. Tonight, he wouldn't say a single word. But just wait. Soon, he would be the teller. Soon, he would land the Alligator King. Soon.

He shifted gears and drove off into the darkness.

The sound of the engine startled Sabine and Ranger. The crack of the rifle had been bad enough, but the truck's engine always brought back memories. It reminded them of the day that

Gar Face had carried the calico and Puck away. The fur stood up on Sabine's back and she hissed.

Ranger waited until the sound disappeared, then walked out to his bowl. He sat down and licked it, even though it was already completely clean. His stomach rumbled. Sabine walked toward him and stretched. She was glad to get out from the Underneath at least. Over the last few days, Gar Face had been too close, hardly leaving the porch.

Sabine was hungry too. She rubbed against Ranger and walked toward the woods. But before she got there, she lifted her nose in the air. A change was coming. Rain. A lot of rain. A storm was on its way.

# 97

DOWN, DOWN, DOWN Puck fell, through the branches of the tupelo, which seemed to claw at him as he passed. Down, down, down, through the humid air. Down, down, down, onto the hard red dirt beside the Little Sorrowful Creek.

*Thud!*

He landed on his feet, as all cats do, but he hit the ground with such force that it smacked all the air out of him. For a moment everything spun, the trees, the pine needles, the water beside him. His ears rang.

He blinked. Coughed. His sides ached from lack of air. He had a long, thin scratch along his right side. His legs felt as though they had been jammed into his spine. He didn't think he could stand up. He rolled over onto his side. He could feel his heart pounding. He panted. Air. He needed some air.

He could hear the water from the creek. It echoed in his ears. *Water. We must be near water.* He coughed again. If only he could catch his breath . . .

If only he could get to the other side of the creek.

If only, if only, if only . . .

*Promise you'll go back.*

More spinning. More echoes. The scratch burned. His legs burned. The lingering boom of the rifle burned. Night began to roll in, dark and silent. The trees whispered among themselves. And Puck, brave Puck, the tumbling creek rolling along beside him, passed clean out.

# 98

IT STARTED AS an oh-so-gentle sprinkling of drops, so fine it might have been only a heavy dew or a thin, thin mist.

Near the tilting house, Sabine hurried back to the Underneath. She had had little luck on her hunt. All of the prey that she depended on had scurried for shelter at the impending storm. Her belly gnawed at her, and she knew that Ranger was even hungrier. All she had to show for her hunt was a small green lizard, hanging from her mouth.

At home, Ranger waited for her, his long ears drooping over his paws.

Meanwhile, at the ratty tavern, Gar Face sat in his dark corner, a bottle of rum on the table in front of him. He leaned back in his chair and smiled. He paid no attention to the sound of the raindrops, small whispers, as they tapped on the tin roof over his head. All he could hear were the tales of the men at the other tables. He soaked them in, stories of fifty-pound catfish, anecdotes of trapped black bears and huge raccoons. But what he wanted to hear about most were the alligators.

Soon, he thought, he'd be the most revered trapper in the piney woods. Gar Face, a man who refused to remember the name his parents gave him, the one he left behind on the wharves of the Houston Ship Channel, left on the floor of his childhood home, right next to his drunken father. Soon the name Gar Face would be known to everyone. Soon. He'd show them.

He took another pull from the tall bottle and sank down into his chair. Outside, the rain came down, harder and harder.

Grandmother spun in her cell. There was a storm on the way. She could tell. Her eyes flashed in the darkness. Lightning flashed in the clouds. *Sssssoooooonnnn* . . .

# 99

AT LAST GAR Face had his fill of other men's stories of bravado and skill. He handed the barkeep a couple of muskrat pelts and walked out to his waiting truck. The rain dripped off the branches of the overhanging trees. He climbed in and drove back onto the overgrown road. Before he drove to the tilting house, however, he veered off in a different direction. Eventually he came to a small meadow, where he pulled over and rolled the window down. The humid air of the night settled on him. From the glove compartment, he pulled out another bottle of rum and set it on the dash in front of him. He leaned back in his seat and smiled. He barely noticed the drops of rain pattering on the windshield and the truck's roof over his head.

He didn't come to this meadow often, his "victory meadow," the place where he had felled the deer when he was just a boy. He had never told anyone about the deer. Who would believe him? Who would care? But he would tell everyone about the alligator.

The meadow was also the only clearing large enough to see stars. When he was a boy in Houston, there were stars aplenty, dim above the city lights. He remembered them. Of course, tonight there were no stars, only rain. It didn't matter. The scattering of drops on the dusty windshield left their own star-shaped imprints. He took a deep draught from the bottle and wiped his mouth with the back of his sleeve. His face was still itchy from his morning with the mosquitoes. But the rum helped to deaden the pain.

It was only a matter of time now; he'd catch the Alligator King. Gar Face. Soon, everyone would know this chosen name, chosen for him by strangers, people who had laughed at him, sneered at his misshapen features. Soon, they'd say that name out loud. Soon.

He chugged back another swallow from the bottle and sank down into his seat. All around him the rain came down, harder and harder.

# 100

ALONG THE BANKS of the creek, Puck stirred. The cold rain pelted down on him and brought him to attention. He stood up just as—*Craaaacckk!* A bolt of lightning split the air. His wet fur stood up. His head felt thick from his earlier fall, and every muscle ached. He looked around. All he could see was the solid night. He felt the pouring rain soak into his coat. He scratched his ear with his back paw. He licked his side. There was a long scratch from his front paw to his back. He could tell it wasn't deep, but it was sore nonetheless.

*Crrrrraaaack!* Another bolt of lightning lit up the woods around him, lit up the tall tupelo tree. All at once, Puck remembered his fall. And so did his sore body. He stretched. He didn't think anything was broken.

And then, as if the lightning were a zipper in the clouds, it opened them up and let the water out. Buckets and buckets of cold rain, sheets of it. Rain that had traveled for thousands of miles, stored in the heavy clouds that now hovered over the piney woods.

Puck hurried for the warm den at the base of the old pine tree. Soaked, he shook off the water and eased his body into a prone position. He ached all over, from nose to tail. Outside, the rain fell and fell and fell some more.

But Puck was safe, safe in his small, dark den. *You'll be safe in the Underneath.* A flood of relief washed over him, but soon enough, the steady beat of the rain whispered into Puck's sore ears ... *Promise. Promise. Promise.*

And deep beneath the little lair, another creature stirred too. *The daughter. I'll take the daughter.*

So many promises.

Only a few feet away, the creek began to rise.

# 101

WHAT SABINE NOTICED the next morning was the sound of the old truck, returning. Next, she heard Gar Face's heavy footfalls as he clumped up the wooden porch steps. She recognized the slam of the screen door. The floor above her head creaked under his weight. These were sounds she had lived with her entire life. They were predictable; they formed a pattern that she used to time her comings and goings.

She listened some more. Turned her ear toward the front of the house. Waited. There! The slam of the screen door again. That meant that Gar Face had remembered to feed Ranger. She relaxed. *This would be a good day.*

She watched as Gar Face set the bowl of chow in front of Ranger. Ranger cowered as the man approached. Often the bowl of food was accompanied by a hard kick and a yelp. She held her breath. The man walked away. He did not kick him or sneer at him or shout at him. Simply set the bowl down. Sabine exhaled.

*Yes, today will be a good day.*

As soon as she heard Gar Face walk back up those steps, heard the door slam, she moved toward the edge of the house. First she slipped her pink nose, little whiskers twitching, into the open. Ahh, the rain, soft and fine, last night's storm made everything feel new and clean.

Old Ranger saw her slipping out. He moved over and let her join him at his food bowl. There wasn't much there, just some stale dog food, the cheapest brand, but he was glad to share it with this small sister, this little gray cat, this daughter of his old friend. The food, the misty rain, the cool air. Despite the weariness that he had recently worn like an old coat, he thought, *Today will be a good day.*

Neither one of them noticed that Gar Face stood on the top step watching them. The slammed door had been a trick. "Bait," he said under his breath. And the Alligator King swam through his thoughts, all one hundred feet of him.

# 102

FOR SABINE, THE rain was a good thing. She stood beside her friend, Ranger, while he chewed on the food in his bowl. It was the sun that was dangerous. But today there was no sun, only this steady rain. Sabine felt it fall softly on her thick fur. It felt fresh and cool. She stood up and shook. This soft rain would loosen the dirt that clung to her from the Underneath. The yard was littered with trash, including old boards. There was one right next to Ranger's food bowl, a board that served as an island in the muddy yard. She sat on it, licked her back right paw. As soon as she was satisfied, she started on the other. This day was starting out just right. A bowl of food for Ranger. The sighing rain.

Soon she was completely absorbed in her personal bath, concentrating fully on licking every strand of her silver fur. She cleaned her paws, including in between her toes. She reached over and licked her narrow back. She tucked her head and cleaned her soft-as-velvet belly. And every few minutes, she stopped and licked Ranger's long ears. He loved it when she did that.

Ranger finished eating the meager meal and rolled over on his side. There in the rain, he rolled onto the muddy ground next to his bowl while Sabine sat next to him on the board. For a moment she felt completely happy. The rain, the food, her old dog. Sabine knew how to catch small moments of happiness, and this was one.

How could she know that Gar Face had not gone into his house, that the slammed door was only a ruse? How could she know that he had seen the Alligator King on the swampy land that rested between the Bayou Tartine and the Petite Tartine? How could she know that his lust for that alligator was bigger than the gator himself? How could she know that he needed fresh bait, a live animal to tie to a rope and set on the bank of the lazy bayou? How could she know that she was perfect? Perfect bait? How could she know that Gar Face had waited, had watched her while she sat next to the old hound, watched her until she curled her legs beneath her body and closed her eyes, so he could sneak up behind her and grab her by the neck, until he had his rough hands around her neck, strangling her, choking her, grabbing her?

She screamed, "Yeoooowwww!"

## 103

ROLLING IN THE mud beside his food bowl, Ranger had failed to hear Gar Face sneak up on his little cat. But one sound leads to another. When Ranger heard Sabine cry, a new sound filled the air, the high-pitched growl of a furious hound.

Hear it. Like the low whine of a chain saw biting into tree bark.

Hear it. A hound gone wild with fury.

Hear it. A hound grown crazy with anger.

Ranger didn't know how many days had passed since he had watched Gar Face stuff the calico cat and her boy kitten into that burlap bag, had thrown them into the back of the pickup truck, the one that leaked a dark puddle of oil onto the ground beside the tilting house, but to him it was like yesterday, like it was only yesterday, that day when he had strained against the chain, pulled at it so hard, cried so long and so hard that his throat became tattered and raw, too raw to sing, to yelp, to bark. Like it was only yesterday since he had uttered anything beyond a whisper to Sabine, or beyond a coarse rasp when the steel-toed boot met his sore ribs. No more than that, a whisper or a rasp, had come from Ranger in all that time.

But when he saw Gar Face lift up his one and only Sabine, the one he loved more than sunlight, more than soup bones, more than the scent of the trail, when he saw the fish-faced man grab her with his rough hands and begin to shake her, Ranger's voice split the air.

His deep snarling and yelping cracked open the wet morning, sent a shiver up the spines of the elms, the oaks, the sycamores.

Caught Gar Face by surprise, and in that moment of surprise, Ranger lunged.

Gar Face stumbled backward, and when he did, he let go of the silver cat. Sabine fell to the ground and gasped. If Ranger had not been snarling and growling, he would have told her to run, run, run. Get away from this evil place, this house with its sorry tilt, this man with his rough hands. But he did not have to say it. Sabine ran. She ran and ran and ran, until she found a low-lying yaupon bush, surrounded by a thick stand of palmetto. The palmetto scratched her face, her sides, her legs, as she darted through it to the yaupon. It was just beyond the terrible yard but far enough away. She would stay there for now, surrounded by palmetto. Hidden from the hideous man.

She did not see Gar Face swing the old board at Ranger's back and miss, did not see him slip in the grimy mud, did not see him hit the ground. She did not see Ranger sink his teeth into Gar Face's leg. But she heard the pain in the man's voice. She also heard the anger. "You'll pay, you blasted dog." She heard the screen door slam. She heard Ranger stop growling. Then, for the first time in a very long time, she heard her old dog lift his head and howl.

*Arrrooooooooo!!*

Sabine listened, clung to his beautiful, strong voice.

*Arrrooooooooooo!!!*

It filled up the piney woods.

*Arrrrooooooooooooo!!!*

She closed her eyes. She had missed his howl for so long, all she wanted to do was sink inside its pure and simple clarity; but then she realized, this was not the howl of his lullaby or even of the blues. Here was a cry of anger. Here was a cry of sorrow. Here, right here, was a howl of pain.

Sabine slumped deeper in her hiding place. Nothing good could come from this.

# 104

NOT FAR AWAY, one wet Puck sat on the bank of the creek all alone and watched the water rise. The creek was twice as wide as it had been the day before. He was still sore from his attempt at squirrel imitation, but he felt better, especially after a breakfast of voles, a pair of them, found beneath a clump of leaves near his den. With the rain slowing down, all the little animals had crept out of their watery nests. Perfect for a sore, hungry cat.

There was hardly any light, so gray was the morning, and the sun was still tucked well inside the clouds. He licked his wet paws. Licked the long scratch on his side. He tucked his paws beneath him and watched the growing creek. He would never get across it now.

As if the creek could hear him thinking, he thought he heard it murmur.

*Sister! Sister! Sister!*

It was almost as though it was calling to him.

*Sister, sister, sister.*

Yes. He had a sister. But Sabine was not here. He closed his eyes and remembered her, his twin, his match. He missed her.

*Sister, sister, sister.*

The Little Sorrowful rolled by. He opened his eyes and looked toward it. A distant crack of thunder rumbled through the treetops. It seems that electricity beckons electricity, for just then a nearby bolt of lightning zipped through the clouds and sizzled right behind him. The air crackled. His whiskers buzzed.

And then, as if the lightning had created a door, an opening, Puck heard a sound he had not heard in such a long time, a howl, a howl that rolled through the charged air.

*Arrrooooooooo!!!*

Puck shook his head.

*Aroooooooooo!*

There it was again!

Could it be? Could it? Was he sure?

*Arooooooooooo!!!*

Puck knew only one hound who had this howl. Rolling through the woods, splitting open the rainy air, drifting onto the banks of the creek where he sat, the howl came right toward him. He cocked his ears. It could only be Ranger!

A huge and sacred Yes surged through Puck's body.

*Arooooooooooo!!!*

There it was again. He cocked his ears to get a better idea of the direction from which it came.

*Arrrooooooooo!*

Just as he had always known, it came from the other side of

the creek. Puck did not think it was far. If he could get to the other side, he knew he could find them. He would take them away from the man with the rough hands, Gar Face. How? He had no idea. Only that he had promised. He cocked his ears again. Puck stood on his back legs, like a rabbit, and waited.

The creek rumbled by, louder now with its rising water. Puck walked in a circle and stood again on his hind legs, as if he could sniff the noise out of the air. He strained his ears.

But there was only silence. He sat down. He heard the creek run and the rain fall, but no more howls, no more songs.

No matter! He knew the direction. If he walked in that direction, east and a little north, he would surely find them. He knew he would.

*Arrrrooooooo!!!*

Puck heard it again. Then he realized this wasn't the same howl that he had heard when he was a baby. This one was urgent, serious, filled with anger. The answer flew at him again. Something awful must have happened.

*Arrrrooooooo!!!*

He had to go.

*Go back, Puck. Promise you'll go back and find your sister.*

*Arroooooo!!!*

There it was again.

*Go back. Promise you'll break the chain.*

They were in danger. Puck knew it. Knew it as a solid truth. Suddenly his nostrils were filled with the old smell of those rough hands. The odor washed over him, those hands that smelled of flesh and bones and something ancient. The smell of the burlap bag, the smell of the gasoline, the smell of the metal truckbed. He could smell it all.

And then, as if to seal the deal, *arrrooooooo!!!* slipped through the pouring rain. Puck looked out across the creek, he panted, his sides heaved in and out, his need to get to the other side was urgent. He knew now exactly in which direction he needed to go, set his cat radar to the sound of Ranger's howl.

# 105

SABINE SHIVERED BENEATH the yaupon bush. She knew that Ranger was in trouble. She could smell it, smell the pungent odor. Trouble. She shook herself as hard as she could to try to repel it. Trouble. It fell onto her back as hard as the drenching rain.

Almost as punctuation, she felt a flash of lightning strike nearby, followed immediately by a loud clap of thunder. It charged her wet fur, made it stand straight up. Trouble. It cornered her.

How long, she wondered, before she could return, could go back to Ranger, crawl under the tilting house, curl up beside him? Surely Gar Face would leave that night, he always did. But night was a long way off. She tucked her paws underneath herself. *I'll wait*, she thought. But as she wrapped her tail around her face, she felt a huge wave of loneliness wrap itself around her too. She and Ranger had never been so far apart. Even when she hunted for mice and crawfish, she hardly ever went more than a hundred feet beyond the yard.

And what about Ranger? Chained to the corner of the house?

She sat straight up. She should go back. She swished her tail from side to side.

What about Ranger?

What about him?

Chained?

What about Ranger?

Trouble.

Trouble.

She could smell it.

What about Ranger?

The question turned into a continuous loop. She knew she could not return until the evening. It was too dangerous. Another bolt of lightning struck only yards away, the thunder cracked the sky wide open. Rain came down in buckets. And only yards away, Gar Face stomped out of the house and grabbed the rusted chain, dragged the snarling dog out from under the tilting house. He had wrapped a dishtowel around the leg that Ranger had bitten, but the blood was seeping through. The pain seared through his calf, added heat to his anger. He pulled at the chain, pulled the dog, twisting and snarling, from the dark, dry Underneath. "Stupid, stupid dog!" he yelled. "I could have used the cat as bait."

Ranger growled. He bared his teeth. But Gar Face laughed, laughed his hideous laugh. "But a dog will work just fine."

And with that, he yanked the terrible rusted chain with one hand, pulling Ranger down into the mud. Then he grabbed the old board that Sabine had sat on only moments before, the one where she cleaned her silver coat, where she reached out and licked Ranger's silky ears. Gar Face grabbed that rotten board, swung it over his head, and brought it down on Ranger's face. *Whack!* The sound was sickening.

Ranger felt the white-hot pain jolt through his jaw, his eye, his ear. The whole side of his face burned. He yelped in pain, but the yelp only made it worse. He tugged against the chain, he tugged and tugged, but Gar Face was a large man, his chest was broad from dipping the pole of his pirogue into the muddy bayou night after night, his legs were strong from years of slogging through the boggy marsh. His arms were thick with muscles from dragging the heavy alligators out of the water and pinning them to the shore.

When Ranger was a young dog, he would have been a match. He would have grabbed the board in his powerful jaws and snapped it in two. He would have lunged for Gar Face's throat and been done with him.

But Ranger was an old dog, a dog who had not had a decent meal in years, a dog whose ribs showed through his skin, whose fur fell out in patches.

He tasted the blood that filled up his mouth and nose, dripped on the ground. His legs trembled so that, beaten and defeated, he crashed into the mud. The mud was cold, but he could hardly feel it. His nose was so full of blood, he could barely breathe. He panted, gasped for air, but his tongue was so thick there was hardly any room for the air to slip past.

Gar Face pulled at the unforgiving chain and dragged the old dog to his feet. "Come on," he yelled, throwing the splintered board across the yard and pulling Ranger toward him. Ranger could feel his eyelids begin to swell shut. He panted for air.

Then he saw Gar Face do something he hadn't seen in years. He unfastened the rusted chain from the corner of the house. A small amount of courage streamed through the beaten dog. Despite the pain, he rose up as tall as he could.

Gar Face yanked on the chain. Ranger walked. Once, he had been the finest bloodhound in the piney woods, on this side of the Sabine River, the silver Sabine that wandered to the sea. Once Ranger had tracked a painter, one of the last in the forest, cornered him against a farmer's fence. He was not afraid of the beast with its yellow eyes and its terrible claws. Ranger had held him there and bayed and bayed and bayed until at last Gar Face had caught up with him and shot it.

Before the incident with the bobcat, there was nothing Ranger couldn't track. And then came that night, that long-ago night when he had paused and Gar Face shot him, shot his own dog in the leg. The wound healed, but his master had forsaken him, chained him to the corner post and left him, left him to walk in interminable circles day after interminable day.

As Ranger limped along behind the man, he thought about all those times when he had found the scent, found the prey. Then he realized: He was a good dog. He was.

Here was a dog who had been faithful all along. Here was a dog who had lifted his voice into the air and sung his heart out. A dog whose silvery notes filled the forest and wrapped itself around the handsome trees, settled on the silent water of the marsh, filled up the humid air of the swamp. Here was a dog who had done his best his whole life.

He sucked in air, choked. Yes, he had done his best. But here also was a dog who had promised to protect a small mother cat and her kittens, who had slept while Gar Face scooped up the mama and her boy cat. Took his very best friend. Took her away, the one who had loved him fully and completely, had entrusted her kittens to his protection. And he had promised, promised, promised. The only one left was Sabine. What had he done for Sabine? He would not have lasted this long without her small offerings of mice and crawdads. Many was the morning when his food dish was left unfilled and she had scampered into the nearby woods to find something for him to eat, a five-lined skink, a fresh frog, even insects. Once she had even brought him a tough old grackle. Nothing had ever tasted better. And he had been grateful, for without them, he would not have eaten on those days. Sabine. And then, in a single unguarded moment, he had failed to protect even her, the one he loved the most. He hoped that she had run far away from this terrible place and this terrible man.

He started coughing, leaving a trail of blood on the muddy ground. Here was a dog with nothing left, nothing except a large and generous heart, a heart that was cracking down the middle with every difficult breath.

He heard the chain rattle in his ear. The chain. He had hated that chain for such a long time. And now Gar Face was pulling him with it, pulling him along the rain-soaked banks of the Bayou Tartine. He lowered his head, just as he had done when he had been on the hunt so many years ago. His broken nose was so battered, he could barely smell anything but the mud, slippery and thick from the rain.

Barely smell anything, not even a small silver cat, a little girl cat, who watched as he passed by and silently slipped behind him, followed him as Gar Face pulled him toward the Bayou Tartine and the hundred-foot beast he dreamed of.

# 106

THERE IS NOT much a tree can do besides stand still under the sun and stars, or bend back and forth in the wind. But here and there, perhaps once every thousand years, those who know trees agree that a tree can, if it chooses, take matters into its own branches. So when the loblolly pine, this pine, saw its kitten, bruised and scratched from his earlier fall, his small ears cocked to the bay of the old hound, the one that sang the blues, whose silvery notes had filled the nighttime air so many times, it knew longing for what it was, an ache that reached right into the very marrow of its thick trunk.

So much water makes the ground softer than soft, so soft that an old tree, one that has stood for centuries, one that was struck by lightning and has dwindled down to less than half its greatest size, whose limbs fell to the earth with a crash, whose long and lovely needles turned coppery red and settled on the mossy ground, whose upper stories cracked off one after another and dropped away, whose trunk split in two and made a nest for one lost kitten, this old tree, this singular loblolly pine, the one that has held an ancient jar in its web of tangled roots for a thousand years, held it deep underground with its even more ancient inhabitant, this very tree finally let go of the soggy earth that had held it all these years and leaned over.

*CRRAAACCKKK!!!*

*SPLLIIIITTTT!!!*

*BOOOMMMMM!!!*

The tree swayed and rocked, and finally, finally fell. And when it did, the roots, like a million fingers, pulled the old jar to the surface, pulled it up, up, up into the dark gray of the wet morning.

And as the jar rose through the silty red dirt, Grandmother Moccasin awoke from her long slumber, leaned against the side, pushed against it until at last the pot tipped over and rolled down the side of the bank. She curled herself into a tight knot and tucked her head into it. *CRAAAACKKK!*

*Ahhh*, she whispered, *at last!*

After a thousand years of solid dark, a small sliver of light slipped into her cavern. A crack, a crack that formed a V, a perfect wedge. She slithered through it, leaving her old layer of skin behind, for it was already too small for her. She had lived in it for all that time, for so many years we hardly know how to count them, just waiting to scrape it off, left it in the old jar, her ancient prison. For the first time in years too numerous to count, rain, cool and sparkling, spilled over her blue-black skin, skin as black as night, so black it seemed blue, so black it gleamed. She paused to look back at her ancient skin and the broken jar and then quietly slipped into the salty water of the Little Sorrowful Creek.

She did not see the silver furred cat, running, like a gray blur, away from the tree. Puck had slipped out of the den just in time to turn around and, in the dim light of dawn, see the old tree that he had called home fall onto its side.

*CRRRAAAASSSHHHHHH!!!*

He did not notice the jar or the snake. He did not notice that the rain was slowing down. He did not notice the way the tree rocked and swayed, back and forth, before it finally fell. All he noticed were his own four legs running beneath him as fast as they could go.

# 107

THE RAIN FALLING into his fur was cold, cold, cold, like the creek. For a moment Puck was frozen. And then he ran, ran, ran as hard as he could, away from the old dead tree, away from the creaking and cracking, away from the deafening noise.

But when he finally stopped, he realized that he had run in the wrong direction, away from Ranger's howl. He had to turn around. He had to go back to where the tree had fallen. He shook from top to tail. From a distant part of the forest, he heard another crack of lightning sizzle through the air. His fur, as wet as it was, stood straight up. The air felt charged; it hummed in his ears.

Slowly he turned and walked back toward the old tree, toward the spot on the bank where he had finally heard Ranger's bay. He could feel the sky stepping back in favor of the lofty branches of the towering trees. And as he walked, he saw the creek beside him, rising ever higher. He would never get across it now. Never.

Suddenly he was overwhelmed by it all. Such a deep and utter Missing. Missing his twin, his match. Missing his Ranger, with his large silky ears, and his furry belly that he used to climb, his lullaby, missing that lullaby. Missing his mama, her calico coat, her rough tongue on his head. Missing.

Now he knew where Ranger and Sabine were, but they might as well be on a different planet. The creek was still in between them. He hung his head and walked. Next to him, the creek tumbled by, frothy with its extra water, excited by the joining of so much rain in its thirsty bed. Even the air was filled with water. Puck felt almost as though he were drowning.

He was so full of Missing that he almost missed the tree.

This tree. This beautiful and sturdy tree.

A tree that has finally crashed to earth twenty-five years after that stray bolt of lightning, twenty-five years after a father in Houston hit a boy in the face, twenty-five years of dying. Here, here in this piney woods is a tree that has spun and spun and spun in the rain-soaked clay that has held it for so long, spun in its last moments, rocked from side to side, and leaned, leaned just so, in just the right direction, at just the right angle, so that it has fallen across the salty creek, the creek this tree has stood beside its whole life long.

Puck looked at the fallen tree. Here at last, right in front of him, was a bridge.

## 108

IT FINALLY HAPPENED. Grandmother was free. Immediately she slid into the salty creek, but she did not stay there for long. After a thousand years of hearing only her own voice, her own beating heart, her own thoughts, she needed to hear the voice of someone familiar.

She quickly slithered across the ground on the opposite side of the creek, reveled in the cool rain pouring onto her new skin, delighted in her ability to stretch to her full length.

Soon she slipped across the old quicksand pit. Another creature might get sucked into it, but not Grandmother. She passed over it so fast that the shivering sands didn't have time to grab her.

At last she arrived at the edge of the large bayou, where she wrapped her sinewy body around an old cypress tree and pulled herself out onto a huge limb that hung over the water. Below, she saw the familiar bubbles rising to the surface.

"Sister!" The alligator rose to the top. She could see that he had grown in both girth and length, and she was impressed.

"I've returned," she said.

"I've been waiting," he replied.

And so he had, waited and waited, all these many years. He had wondered where she had gone, where she had hidden all this time, but he had also known that she would return. "You've been gone a long time," he said.

"Where is she?" hissed the snake. "The daughter!"

But just as he started to give her the news, all thousand years of it, he smelled someone approaching. Ahh, the man! And with that, the Alligator King flipped his tail and sank into the water. Grandmother could wait. *What is a day*, he shrugged, *in the eye of a thousand years?*

Unhappy, Grandmother slithered up the old cypress, as far up as she could go, into the uppermost branches, wrapped herself around a limb, and hissed. *Ssssstttttt!!!* From her sky-high vantage point, she watched.

## 109

BACK ON THE other side of the creek, Puck moved a little closer to the tree bridge. He could smell the water. He could feel the spray of it in his nose. He took a few more steps. He walked out onto the broad back of the tree. *Whoosh*, the water tumbled beneath him, carrying small branches with it, churning as it went. This was not the same quiet creek he had splashed in with the turtles only days earlier. That had been bad enough. This was much, much worse. The tree swayed from the water's impact against its side. Water splashed in front of him and behind him. He could tell it was rising quickly. If he did not get across soon, the tree would be underwater, and he would be swept along with it.

He looked down and saw an eddy, swirling in a large and rapid circle. The smell overwhelmed him. Water in his nose. In his ears.

*Go back. Go back. Go back.*

Puck shook his head. He took another step. His legs wobbled underneath him. He looked down. The water was coursing by. He felt queasy. He felt dizzy. He felt his stomach churn. He took another deep breath.

*Go back. Promise. Go back.*

Then he ran. Ran to the other side. He did not wait. He ran. And the old tree, a thousand years old, free at last from standing in one place for such a long time, buckled in half and fell into the tumbling creek.

# 110

FINALLY ON THE other side, Puck felt disoriented. The rain had diminished, becoming first a drizzle and then a fine mist. He stopped for a moment to readjust his radar and aim his body in the direction of Ranger's howl. He pointed his ears toward the north and a little to the west.

He listened. He waited.

But there was no sound other than the creek behind him and the growing chorus of birds stepping out of their nests before the rains returned. Puck looked up. The rain had stopped, but the sky was still gray. It would return. He had to hurry. He knew he was not far now from his sister, from his Ranger, from the dark Underneath where he was born.

There are stories of cats who have traveled thousands of miles to return to the places of their birth. Puck did not have to travel that far. As the crow flies, it was probably less than two miles between the tilting house where he was born and his pine tree den. On the ground, it was probably a little farther. But Puck's line was fairly straight, so maybe no more than a quarter mile could be added to the journey.

As soon as Puck walked up to the tilting house, saw the littered yard, the rusted pickup truck with its dark puddle of oil beneath it, that truck that had carried him and his mother away, as soon as he breathed in the rancid air, full of rotten fish and flesh and the decrepit outhouse that sat on the far edge of the property, as soon as he saw the rickety steps and the old bottles and cans that littered the place, his stomach surged. He could taste the bile in his mouth.

*Go back! Go back! Go back!*

Those two words! They repeated themselves over and over.

But then he looked at the scene in front of him and realized, this *was* back. He had promised. He had nodded his head. He had told his mother he would go back, go back for Sabine and Ranger.

Sabine and Ranger.

He crept low and walked toward the porch. He was forced to use his mouth in order to breathe, so noxious was the air around him. His fur stood on end. He got as low to the ground as possible and crawled toward the porch. From where he was, on the edge of the yard, he could see the space underneath, see the deep and holy dark. His whiskers twitched.

Here was an open space between his spot in the woods and the edge of the porch. It was only twenty feet or so, but to Puck it seemed like a mile. There was no cover between here and there. He would have to take extreme caution.

He crouched even closer to the muddy ground, could feel it

on his belly as he moved forward. Every muscle tensed. His tail twitched. Closer, closer, closer.

Finally he whispered, "Sabine!" Closer. "Sabine!" Another step. "Sabine!" There was no answer. Another step. Perhaps she couldn't hear him. He was only a few feet away now. He took a deep breath and . . . *spring!* He darted into the Underneath.

"Sabine!" he called in his loudest whisper.

It took him a moment for his eyes to adjust to the dark. He sat down. Nothing had changed. It was exactly the same as he remembered, except that the ceiling seemed a little lower and the old boot that he had hidden in when he was a baby seemed a little smaller. He sat down. Standing here, in this place where he was born, he could almost hear Ranger's song, barely detect the words. . . .

*No need to cry, no need to fear . . .*
*When those ol' sunbeams break the day*
*I will keep you while you play.*

The song rolled around in his head, settled in his memory.

He stood in the middle of the dark Underneath, this place he had missed all these days, all this time. Now here he was, all alone with only the memory of the song beside him. The tender words settled in his fur.

*No need to cry, no need to fear*
*I will always be right here.*

Puck realized. It was that last line he had clung to. All this time, he had relied on Ranger to *be right here*. And now he wasn't. Where was the hound? Where was Sabine? Surely they couldn't be far away. Hadn't he just heard Ranger's howl only a short time ago?

Puck peered out into the yard, and there, where it had always been, was Ranger's food dish. He quickly crept out and ran to the dish. But he was not met with a bowlful of food. Instead, he was met with a puddle of blood. Even the hard rain had not been able to wash away the unmistakable stains of blood all around. Puck lifted his paw. It was soaked in blood. He looked around. Blood. It was all around him, on the ground, in the bowl, sitting in pools mixed with rain. He shook his paw, shook it hard. Blood sprayed off of it.

The answer came flying at him once more: Something awful must have happened. A sob welled up in his throat. This was his fault. Here was a cat who had broken the rules and now something terrible had happened.

A knot formed in his stomach.

A knot of revulsion.

A knot of fear.

A knot of anger.

Puck started to pant. He could hardly breathe from the impact of the terrible knot. He put his nose to the ground. The blood was clearly Ranger's. But there were two different scents. Someone else was bleeding too. He looked up. The trail was thick, the trail of blood, the same blood that soaked into his fur.

He shook his drenched paw again. He would find the one who did this. He began to walk due east, following the scent of Ranger's blood, and some other blood he didn't recognize, east toward the Bayou Tartine and the swamp that rested between its wide banks and the smaller ones of the Petite Tartine.

## III

GAR FACE TUGGED at the old hound. The dog coughed, and every few feet he stumbled. No matter. The man pulled at the chain. He would drag him if he had to. He looked at the pathetic animal. He had done a number on him, all right. Gar Face smiled. The Alligator King would not be able to resist.

But every few steps, he had to stop and rest his own damaged leg. The hound had taken more out of him than he cared to admit. He looked down at the dirty dish towel. The blood was seeping through. He would tighten it when they got to the spot where the Petite Tartine split off from the main bayou. It wasn't far, perhaps another half mile.

Gar Face grimaced. Stupid hound. He had been bitten by other animals. He held out his hand. There were scars from the many alligators that had clamped down on him while he wrestled them to their deaths. He had been bitten by the sharp teeth of a squirrel and a rat, and more than once he had gotten his fingers caught by the razor teeth of the gar for which he was named. He had even been bitten by a copperhead, a bite that made him sick for over a week, so sick he could not get out of his ratty cot. He was surprised several days later when he woke up to find himself still alive.

But this bite, this bite to his leg by his very own dog, ached in a different way from all those other bites. If Gar Face had been smarter, if he had been at all tuned in to the ways of animals, he might have understood that all those other bites were made in self-defense. Ranger's bite was made out of anger, out of fury, out of protecting someone he loved. There was a difference. But Gar Face was not smarter. Instead he limped, pulled the old dog on the chain, and muttered, "Stupid dog."

In the meantime, Ranger put all his concentration on his steps. One paw, then another. Step. Step. Step. Each one was painful. Each step burned his chest as he gasped for air. He kept his nose to the ground. All he smelled now was the blood from Gar Face's wound. His own blood dripped onto the ground, leaving a trail, yes, leaving a trail for Puck.

# 112

SABINE, SMALL SABINE, she followed her old dog Ranger, stayed as close as she dared without the awful man noticing her. Every few steps he stopped and looked over his shoulder or down at his leg. She knew he might see her, might scoop her up again in his rough hands. She slipped back and forth across the trail, well enough behind, but close enough to keep up. She was the panther, she was the cougar, she was the lioness.

Sabine, small Sabine.

From her nest in the cypress tree, Grandmother Moccasin coiled her huge body around the highest limb and waited. For a thousand years she had waited. She could wait a little longer. She knew that soon enough the Alligator would emerge from the bayou and answer her question: Where was the daughter?

*Yesssssss!!!* she hissed. *I'll take her for my own.*

# 113

BY THE TIME Gar Face reached the spot on the banks where the Bayou Tartine spit off its little sister, the Petite Tartine, the bite wound on his leg throbbed. He reached into his hip pocket and pulled out a flask, tilted back his head, and took a long draught of the rum that he drank for breakfast, lunch, and dinner. If he drank enough of it, it would numb the pain from the hound's bite. He wiped his mouth with his arm and took another pull. He had not slept since the day before, and the long walk from the tilting house to this spot on the bayous had left him worn.

There was an old cypress tree along the banks. Many times he had sat right there, under that tree. His pirogue was tied to one of its many knees poking up through the water. But the trunk of the tree itself was ten feet up on the marshy bank. Here was where he'd wait for the Alligator King. The rain was still sliding out of the sky, and he was tired of being wet. The tree offered some small amount of shelter. He pulled the ragged dog to the edge of the bank.

"Sit, you stupid dog," and Ranger, without a single ounce

of energy left, sat down. Then Gar Face walked away, holding the end of the chain.

A man like Gar Face does not go into the swamp without a gun. The rifle was the only thing of value that he owned, the only symbol of a human connection. He lifted the strap over his head and took the rifle off his back. Then he leaned against the trunk of the tree and sank down, setting the rifle on the ground. It was hard to tell the time of day without the sun, but Gar Face knew that it might be hours before the enormous alligator rose up out of the water to feed. Normally alligators feed at night.

He would wait. He hooked the chain around the tree and looked at Ranger, now on his side by the water. "Perfect bait," he said. Then he congratulated himself on his perfect plan. He looked at the wasted dog. "Perfect," he said again. Then he took another deep draught of the rum and slumped down the trunk of the tree. "Perfect," he mumbled once more as he closed his eyes.

Ranger didn't hear him. Every inch of his body was wreathed in a halo of pain. He sucked in air, sucked it past his swollen tongue. His nose was now completely shut. He knew that the gator would come sooner or later. He had been on hunts for gators. Had seen Gar Face stake out an animal, just as he was now staked out. He knew that the blood dripping from his mouth would lure the beast eventually. He only hoped it would be fast. And like the man slumped against the tree, the old dog closed his eyes.

A dog who has been beaten with a board, who has walked over

a mile on legs that trembled with pain, who has gasped for air with every step, deserves something kind, doesn't he? A dog who has been true to those he loved, and even the one he didn't, who did his job without complaint, should have some comfort in the midst of so much misery. Such a dog is worthy of this much. Of something sweet. When Sabine saw that Gar Face was sound asleep, she slipped out from her hiding place and curled up under one of Ranger's long silky ears. She purred to him as hard as she could. She licked the side of his soft face, licked the blood off his nose, she put her nose next to his nose. She loved him as hard as she could. With all her might, she loved Ranger.

He tried to lift his head, to lick her with his long tongue, but the effort was too great. He needed to tell her to go, to leave right away, that she should not be here. To stay would be too dangerous. That's what he needed to tell her, but he could not. Instead he listened to her soft purrs and forgot about how hard it was to breathe.

And then he heard something else, something besides Sabine's gentle purrs. It was a whirring sound, like a bee but softer. He cracked open a swollen eye. A hummingbird! In the late afternoon rain, the little bird glimmered, a tiny rainbow in his battered vision.

Ranger sighed. He could feel Sabine purring under his ear.

From her perch in the tree, Grandmother looked down. A man! While in her jar, she had vowed to stay away from humans, vowed to have no more truck with humankind. Now here was one just below her. Her stomach growled. She was hungry, but the man was too big even for her massive jaws. She would wait for something smaller, something that did not smell so bad. She was good at waiting.

# 114

AS PUCK REACHED the confluence of the two bayous, he saw a hummingbird just in front of him. Up up up it went. Zigging and zagging, brilliant in the rainy sky. He had seen one before, often. A hummingbird. But this time it was so close, he could hear the frantic whirring of its wings.

He trotted after it, mesmerized, but the tiny bird cast a parting shot of light and flew up into the branches of the cypress tree. Anyone who knows cats knows that they are easily distracted when there is zigging and zagging in their paths. Even a cat on a mission. Puck was no exception. All that zigging and zagging hypnotized him; he was entranced by it, spellbound. Without thinking, Puck climbed the old tree after it. But as soon as he climbed into one of the lower branches, the bird disappeared. Puck looked down. He hissed.

There, at the foot of the tree, slumped against its thick trunk, Gar Face. Puck felt the anger rise in his chest. He looked at the evil man, the man who had picked him up with his rough hands that smelled of fish and bones. Then he noticed the leg with the wound. The blood. It was Gar Face's blood that he had smelled besides Ranger's.

He followed the line of sight, saw the old chain, the hated chain tied to the tree. And then, not ten feet away, there they were. Ranger! Sabine!

He started to jump down, to run to them, aching to lick Ranger's long ears, to wrap his paws around Sabine and lick her face, her nose, her ears. His twin. His match. He started to do all this, but then he remembered—Gar Face.

There was something else, too, the rifle. The fur on his back stood up. He needed to get to Ranger and Sabine without waking Gar Face. But how?

He crawled farther out onto the branch to get a better look at the situation. He did not see Grandmother Moccasin, curled tightly around the branch just above his. He did not see her skin so black it looked blue, did not see her slowly uncoil her long body. Puck did not see Grandmother. All he saw was Sabine and Ranger and the terrible man at the foot of the tree.

# 115

A SNAKE WHO has lived in a jar for a thousand years knows something about hunger. She has been hungry for all that time. And now, just beneath her, on a lower branch, sat a small gray cat. She also noticed the little sister, tucked beneath the silky ear of the old hound. She saw the awful rise and fall of the dog's chest. She took note of the cat on the branch below, took in his huge and hungry longing. Silently, she moved down toward the small, tasty cat on the branch.

Just beneath the surface of the bayou, the Alligator King was hungry too. He heard the soft tapping of the rain on the water. The dark clouds above made it seem later than usual. And this made him hungrier than usual. He knew that the man was waiting for him on the bank. He had smelled him coming. But he did not expect the man to be so quiet. What was he waiting for? As the alligator raised his snout above the water, he noticed the pleasing odor of blood. Perfect. He followed the scent, held closely on the air. He had known the man would bring an animal to use as bait. A canine would do. But then he took another sniff. *Ahhh*, he thought, *even better. There are two!*

## 116

THE RAIN FELL, becoming denser. From the low branch of the cypress, Puck squinted his eyes to see through the heavy drops. He did not know that there was an enormous snake slowly making her way from the branches above, heading directly for him. All of his attention was directed toward his sister and the old hound.

Below he saw the top of Gar Face's head, leaning against the trunk. He had to get to Sabine without disturbing the foul-smelling man.

But it was too late. Just as Puck began his slow descent down the trunk of the tree, Gar Face stirred. Puck saw him wipe his nose with the back of his hand. Saw him push himself up and shake his head. Saw him grab his rifle. Saw him look toward Ranger. Heard him say, "Well, lookee here. The cat came back." Saw him aim the rifle in Sabine's direction. Saw Sabine freeze.

Puck saw Gar Face close one eye to center his target, saw him curl his finger on the trigger. Something terrible was about to happen.

The knot of anger in Puck's belly tightened. He would not let Gar Face harm his sister. When the little cat saw Gar Face aim the rifle at his sister and his hound, he opened his mouth and yowled at the top of his lungs.

*Yeeeeeeoooooooowwwwwww!!!*

Gar Face jumped at the piercing sound and jerked his rifle up, in the direction of the noise, up toward the limbs of the cypress tree, up toward Puck and the enormous snake moving toward him, up, up, up.

He pulled the trigger.

*BOOM!!!*

For the second time in his life, Puck let go of his limb and dropped, dropped out of the tree, dropped right onto that hideous face that looked like the ancient fish he was named for.

"Aaaaaaaarrrrrrrrrrggggggghhhhhhh!" Gar Face howled. The pain was excruciating, pain even more pronounced and sharp than the bite on his leg, still seeping through the dirty towel. Gar

Face screamed as the gray cat dropped onto his face with all his claws extended. He threw the rifle toward the bayou. With both hands he pulled the cat off his face, losing more skin in the process. Then, gripping Puck by the neck, he ran the ten feet to the Bayou Tartine. He held on to the cat with one hand, dipped his other into the bayou and cupped the cool water onto his face, his burning face. He was blinded by the pain.

Blood dripped into the water. He slowly opened his eyes. The last thing Gar Face ever saw was the open mouth of the Alligator King, waiting, waiting, waiting, there on the edge of the Bayou Tartine. Saw the rows of razor-sharp teeth, the strong jaws, open, open, open, felt them close around his neck. And as the Alligator King twisted Gar Face, spun him once, twice, three times in the murky water, darkness, solid and thick, fell.

# 117

WHEN GAR FACE threw Puck and his mother into the Little Sorrowful Creek so long ago, the water had been harsh and unforgiving, making Puck gasp and choke, but here in the bayou, the water all around felt cool and inviting. It soothed the soreness around his neck where the man had choked him. And when the man let go, the water wrapped itself around Puck, soft, tender. He felt as though he were floating, floating, floating.

He opened his eyes and saw a million bubbles. They were beautiful, so many bubbles. He loved the bubbles. So shiny. He could hear them popping all around him. But that wasn't all he heard. As he floated, there was another voice, a familiar voice.

*Swim, Puck. Swim.*

Ahh, that voice. His mother's voice. It sounded so close.

*Swim. Swim. Swim.*

It was there, right in his ear. He could hear it more clearly. *Swim. Swim. Swim.* And then the other word from his mother, *promise.*

He started to sink. He could feel himself going down, his mother's words echoing in his ear. Then he heard the words again. *Swim, Puck, swim!* Only this time, it wasn't the voice of his mother he heard. It was someone else. Someone familiar, as familiar as his own skin.

*Swim, Puck, swim!*

It was Sabine. His sister!

*Swim!* she called.

Oh, he had missed Sabine. So much missing.

*Swim!* There was her voice again, growing fainter, dimmer. He was sinking into the missing. He didn't think he could miss her any more.

Then he realized.

Sabine.

She was there, waiting for him.

*Swim!* she called.

And he did.

He swam.

# 118

IT TOOK A while for Puck to catch his breath, but when he did, he looked right into the face of Sabine, a face so like his own. He touched her nose with his nose. He rubbed his forehead against her forehead. He rested his chin on her soft back. Then he wrapped his paw around Sabine's neck and licked her face, her ears, the top of her head. And Sabine reached up and licked Puck's chin, his nose, even his whiskers.

And just like that, a fresh breeze sifted through the forest, the trees shuddered, and the rain stopped. Puck looked up through the branches to see the clouds moving past. And what do you know? The sun. Goldy and warm. The sun came out.

Puck had kept his promise to his calico mother. He looked at his sister, his twin, his match. He had honored his sacred binding.

Together they walked over to Ranger, where Puck leaned against the hound, his beloved old Ranger, heard the beating of his old dog's heart, a heartbeat as familiar as his own.

He curled up next to Ranger and listened to the wonderful thump of that heart, and all at once Puck couldn't keep his eyes open. Exhaustion rolled over him. But just before he drifted off, Ranger stirred, and Puck heard something else familiar, the old rattle of the rusted chain.

# 119

A CAT WHO followed a trail of blood, a dog who was beaten with a board, and another cat who served as witness even though her heart was broken, all of them needed sleep. But there were dangers in sleeping too hard and too long. Who would look out for them? Who would stand watch?

Only once every thousand years or so, give or take a century, do the trees call up their own sort of magic. When they looked upon their tiny twins curled up next to the old and tattered hound, they realized then and there that sleep was called for. So they did what they could to help and stirred up the old Zephyrs of Sleep, just as they had for Night Song and Hawk Man so long ago. Sleep, glorious sleep, it settled over the land between the Tartine sisters, that land of shifting sands. It wafted its way into the nests of the muskrats and beavers. Sleep, silent sleep, it fell upon the crickets and hoot owls, the foxes and turtles and peepers. It curled up on the skins of the million snakes, the kings and corals and copperheads . . . and one other, Grandmother Moccasin . . . sleep wound its way around her, too.

Through the late afternoon, all along the early evening—past the dark of night and into the tender slipping of dawn—the forest, deep and thick, and all of its denizens small and large and in between—all of them—slept.

# 120

MORNING WAS IN full bloom when Puck finally opened his eyes. He stood up and looked over Ranger's shoulder. All night he and Sabine had curled up against him. All night they had snuggled right next to the old dog's chest, just under his ears.

Sabine noticed that sometime in the night, the dog's breathing had become easier, less erratic. Maybe, she hoped, he would be all right. She stood next to her brother and looked at the hound. His face was swollen and there was dried blood running from the edge of his mouth. One eye was swollen shut. She winced. It hurt to look at him.

As she watched, she heard a small sigh escape from his mouth. That seemed like a good thing somehow. Right away, Sabine busied herself with cleaning him up as best she could. Puck joined her. Together, the two licked the dog's wrinkled face and long ears.

Ranger hovered. He could feel the scratchy tongues of his kittens. Nothing had ever felt finer. He cracked open one eye. There, straight in front of him, was a hummingbird. She shimmered in the morning light.

The sight of the bird made him blink. He looked again, but she was gone. In her place a kitten, his kitten . . . and another! Was he seeing double? He lifted his head and blinked his one good eye. There was Sabine, looking back at him.

And yes! Oh yes! There *was* another, sitting right beside her! Was it possible? Did he dare to believe it? He looked again. He saw Sabine, little Sabine, true as could be. But when he looked at the other cat, there it was, the crescent moon on his forehead.

It was Puck!

A surge of happy streamed through the old dog. The pain felt smaller, the bruises and cuts, the bullet in his leg, were diminished in all the happy. He leaned over and licked Puck with as much slobber as he could muster.

But his happiness was dampened. Where was the man? The man with the face like the prehistoric fish, Gar Face? He scanned the banks by the bayou, but all he saw was the old rifle, half in and half out of the water. At once, Ranger knew what had happened. He lowered his head. There was no celebration in this loss of life, even for one such as Gar Face. You might think that as cruelly as the man had treated Ranger, that the dog might feel something like satisfaction, or even joy, at his demise.

But the truth is, the dog didn't feel anything at all beyond relief, relief that the man was finally gone.

He turned away and looked at his two kittens.

Here was his family.

One old hound and two gray kittens.

# 121

BUT HERE ALSO was a chain. Fastened to a tree. And somewhere at the bottom of the Bayou Tartine was an alligator one hundred feet long who would be hungry again soon. Puck looked at the old, rusted chain. He sniffed it. The odor made him recoil. It smelled like the tilting house, like old bones and fish and something rotten.

He licked it, but the cold, metallic taste made him spit. It left small flakes of rust on his tongue. He gagged. He tapped it with his paw and tried to scratch it with his claws. It was solid.

He stared at it hard, walked along its length between Ranger and the tree. It was covered in rust, and there were a couple of places where the links appeared thinner than others. He sniffed it again; the smell was the same.

At last he put his ear against it and listened. He sat there for a long time. Whenever Ranger moved, the chain made a bright, rustling noise. But when Ranger was still, the chain was silent.

Silence. Puck listened.

More silence. And then . . . *sssssssttttttttt!!!*

Puck looked up. There in front of him, her face only inches

from his face, was a creature as old as the seven seas, as old as the swamp, as old as time itself. Her scales gleamed in the morning light. Every inch of Puck's small body buzzed. He couldn't move. She was enormous, as thick around as a small tree. He watched as she glared at him. Behind him, he heard Ranger growl, but he knew that Ranger was no match for the beast in front of him. He felt Sabine walk up beside him, push her body next to his. For one brief moment he thought about running. But he knew that there was no running for Ranger. He looked at his sister. She would not leave either.

He took a deep breath, tried to scream, but no sound came out.

# 122

GRANDMOTHER LOOKED AT the trio in front of her. They were raggedy and spent, especially the dog. The ache she felt inside was sharp. She wound her massive body into a coil in front of them, never taking her eyes off of them, trapping them in her stare. She could taste the poison pooling in her mouth.

*Three,* she thought. She had witnessed three before. All bound together by love.

Love. *Sssssttttttt!!!* What price had she paid for love?

A husband lost to another. A daughter lost to a man. A thousand years trapped in a jar. She stared at the tattered trio in front of her, the two gray cats and the dog chained to the tree. A price. She curled her tail underneath her and flicked her thin black tongue.

Morning widened its arms, grew lighter. She could see them more clearly now, and she watched as the three stood motionless, here, right here beside the Bayou Tartine. She knew that the Alligator King was nearby. Knew that he could return any moment. She smiled. *Sssssooooooonnnn,* she said. But as soon as she said it, she heard a buzz in the humid air. She lifted her head. There, the voices of her reptile cousins, the rattlers, the massasaugas, the Eastern hognose.

*Ssssiiiisster*, their voices rang out.

It was an old call, first heard so long ago, on that day she had swum up the silver Sabine, the warm river to the east, swum here, to this thick and solemn forest.

For a flicker of a second, she took her eyes off her captives and looked up into the greenly trees, saw the small patches of blue sky resting in their upper branches, noticed the sunlight falling in puzzle pieces on the ground all around her. She had missed this. The venom that slid down her throat was sharp and bitter. She swallowed hard, returned her deadly gaze to the three in front of her.

The price!

*Sssssiiiiisssstterrrr!*

Again the cousins called, the rat snakes, the corn snakes, the black and orange corals. She flicked her tongue into the air, tasting the morning dampness that hovered above her blue-black scales, scales the shape of diamonds, scales that looked like mirrors aglow in the thin shards of sunlight dancing on the forest floor. A sharp pang shot through her. There was a price!

*Sssiiiiisssster!*

Their voices buzzed in her ears, the forest hummed. Her body throbbed. She whipped her vicious tail behind her and rose up into the air. She had paid a price.

She looked again at the threesome in front of her. Three

bound by love. And all around the cousins called and called and called.

*Sssssiiiisssttteeerrrr!!!*

*Yes*, she thought, *I know a thing or two about love*. And with that, she opened her steel-trap jaws and struck!

# 123

DEEP UNDER THE water of the muddy bayou, the Alligator King belched. He settled onto the bottom. Through the murk, he saw his old friend swim toward him.

"Sister," he said, and smiled, "your time has come." He had seen her snap the rusted chain in two with her vicious jaws.

"You surprised me," he said.

And so she had. Grandmother, who had spent a thousand years in a jar, had finally chosen love. She had seen it, pure and simple and clean, seen it in the small beings of two gray cats and an old dog. Love in all its complexity and honor made a circle around them all.

She had interfered with love before and caused only sorrow. That, she knew, was the price. This time, she did what she could to help it along. She had snapped the chain in two, setting the old dog loose.

She gave a final good-bye to the Alligator King, thanked him for his long and steadfast friendship. Then she swam to the surface of the bayou, slipped out and slithered back into the large cypress tree. The pain she felt was palpable. There was an enormous hole right in the middle of her sleek black body, the bullet burned inside of her, the bullet she had taken when the man jerked his gun toward the cat's piercing scream.

At last, after thousands of years, her time had come. She looked up. The sunlight sifted down through the branches and soaked into her blue-black skin. She could see the sky, the deep and beautiful blue sky.

As she lay there, wrapped around the branch, she heard the rapid beating of wings. She looked over. There was the hummingbird, aglow in the afternoon sun. Glimmering.

The snake looked at the tiny bird. She looked familiar. She had seen this little one before. Then, all at once, she knew. "Granddaughter!" She sighed.

"Yes," said the tiny bird, "I've been looking for you."

High above, a solitary hawk caught the breeze and cried, *"Screeeeee!!!"* Then he disappeared into the clouds.

# 124

FOR TREES, STORIES never end, they simply fold one into another. Where one begins to close, another begins to open, so that none are ever finished, not really. For Puck and Sabine and Ranger, this old story was the beginning of their new one.

After Grandmother snapped the chain that had bound Ranger to the man for so many years, the small family walked away from the Bayous Tartine and the dangerous spit of land that sat between them.

Where are they now, Puck, Sabine, and Ranger?

If you walked into this old and forgotten forest, you would know they did not return to the tilted house with its yard of bones and skins, gone now, struck by a bolt of lightning that zipped from the darkened sky and burned it completely away, a fire so hot it left only a mound of dark, black coals that simmered and seethed for days afterward. No, they would not be there.

Nor would you see them at the base of the old tree, the loblolly pine that stood for a thousand years, all of it gone, washed away in the Little Sorrowful, that creek made of tears, carried downstream to the silver Sabine, and delivered at last to the beautiful blue Gulf of Mexico.

Nevertheless, they are here.

If you could ask the trees about them, the sweet gums and tupelos, the sycamores and oaks, oh, if only you could decipher the dialects of tallow and chestnut and alder, they would tell you that here, in this lost piney woods, this forest that sits between the highways on the border of Texas and Louisiana, here among the deer paths and giant ferns, along the abandoned trails of the Caddo, here in this forest as old as the sky and sea, live a pair of silver twins and an old hound who sings the blues, right here . . .

Puck . . .

Sabine . . .

. . . and Ranger.

Here.

# ACKNOWLEDGMENTS

A novel does not happen all by itself. It takes a village, and I am blessed to have a host of villagers who took time out of their lives to read this story in all of its incarnations. Many thanks go to my mother, Pat Childress, who just never stops believing; Rose Eder, who would not let Ranger die; Diane Linn, oh wise and wonderful soul that she is, who consistently believed in Grandmother; Donna Hanna Calvert, bearer of light and wonder; Daren Appelt, timekeeper as well as the brother I always wanted; Debbie Leland, who can see things that others can't.

Many others helped along the way as well, including Kimberly Willis Holt, Jeanette Ingold, Rebecca Kai Dotlich, Lola Schaeffer, Marion Dane Bauer, Adrienne Ross, Candice Ransom, Cynthia and Greg Leitich Smith, Laura Ruby, Anne Bustard, and Mary Mansoorian. Alison McGhee sent me small messages of encouragement through every draft.

Could I ever have written this without my students and colleagues at Vermont College? Absolutely not.

I doubt very much that this book would ever have seen the light of day without the wise counseling of Dennis Foley, who told me early on that this was Puck's story; and Tobin (M. T.) Anderson, who said, I'll never forget this, "Write what you think you can't."

I'm also grateful to the folks at Caddo Mounds State Park, outside of Athens, Texas, for taking time to talk to me about the mysterious and wondrous Caddo, who inhabited the woodland areas of East Texas for thousands of years, who were master craftspeople and still are.

If you think that a book can be written without considerable hand-holding, you would be mistaken. My agents, Emily E. Van Beek and Holly McGhee, kept telling me to push, push, push. And I did, even though it was messy and sometimes painful.

And then there is my editor, Caitlyn Dlouhy, who is the resident seer, curandera, and asker of perfect questions. Medicine woman.

A writer needs people in her life who believe in her, even when the dishes in the sink are dirty and she stays tucked away in her cave for hours on end. I have those people—my two handsome sons, Jacob and Cooper, and my sweet and beautiful husband, Ken. They are the melody to my song. They are.

# READING GROUP GUIDE

An abandoned calico cat, about to have kittens, hears the lonely howl of a chained-up hound dog deep in the backwaters of the bayou, and sets out to find him. When they finally meet, Mama the calico cat and Ranger the bloodhound form a fast and unlikely bond, forged in loneliness and fueled by fierce love. They become a family after the kittens are born, and Ranger urges Mama to remain under the porch and raise Sabine and Puck, because Gar Face—the evil man living inside the house—will surely use her or her kittens as alligator bait should he find them. They'll be safe in the Underneath . . . as long as they stay there.

But in a moment of curiosity, one of the kittens sets off an astonishing chain of events that reverberates through the bayou, and brings the past together with the present in remarkable ways. Following the tradition of Marjorie Kinnan Rawlings, Flannery O'Connor, and Carson McCullers, in *The Underneath* Kathi Appelt spins a harrowing yet keenly sweet tale filled with many absorbing themes, such as the power of love (and of hate), the fragility of happiness, and the importance of making good on your promises. This guide is designed to assist your discussion of this poignant novel.

## PRE-READING ACTIVITY

1. The action in the book takes place in the marshy swampland and deep forests of Texas's bayou region. Research bayous and their ecosystems and prepare a report. In what parts of the

world do bayous exist? What kinds of plants and animals live in bayous? How are bayous similar to and different from other ecological environments—for example, what do bayous have in common with the Florida Everglades, and how do the two areas differ?

2. Long before the Europeans settled along the Gulf Coast, a varied group of Native Americans live in the piney woods of East Texas and Louisiana. They were collectively known as the Caddo. It was from the Caddo language that the name for the state of Texas came about. The name meant "friend." In fact, the Caddo were known as a friendly people. Even though Hawk Man and his family weren't Caddo themselves, they might have been welcome in a Caddo village, just as the later Europeans were welcomed. Research the Caddo. There are hardly any left in their original homeland, and they have mostly settled in Oklahoma and Mexico. Why did they leave? What were some of the things that they were famous for? How did they learn to survive in the marshy swamps of their native territory?

## DISCUSSION TOPICS

1. Grandmother Moccasin and her daughter Night Song are lamia, half-serpent and half-human. Hawk Man is also an "animal of enchantment" (page 61), having been a bird before turning into a man. If you could be a shape-shifter, which animal would you choose to become? What do you think of the

shape-shifter rule: "Once a creature of enchantment returns to its animal form, it cannot go back" (page 47)? If you were Hawk Man or his daughter, would you have become an animal again, even if it meant you could never return to your human form?

2. Until he meets Mama the calico cat, Ranger the bloodhound doesn't realize how lonely he is; Ranger muses that when Mama found him "he didn't know that he needed to not be so solitary until at last he wasn't," (page 30). What are the differences between being alone, and being lonely? Is it possible to be lonely even when you're surrounded by people?

3. Abused as a child and later abandoned by his father, Gar Face the trapper lives in a world of anger, and his drinking only deepens his hatred. Does anything make Gar Face happy? If so, what is it? Even though he does evil things throughout the book, do you think he deserved to die in the jaws of the Alligator King?

4. When an author assigns human characteristics to non-human beings, this is called anthropomorphism. What are some examples of anthropomorphism in the book? In real life, do you think plants or animals have feelings like human beings do?

5. Sabine the kitten is named for the Sabine River that feeds the Bayou Tartine. Her brother's name is the same as the playful character in Shakespeare's play, *A Midsummer Night's Dream*— Puck is a mischievous spirit who often gets into trouble. What

do the names of some the characters in *The Underneath*— like those of the kittens, Gar Face, Ranger, Night Song— reveal about their personalities? Does your name have a special origin, or are you named for a family member? How does your name reflect who you are?

6. Ranger, Mama, Sabine, and Puck refer to themselves as a family. What makes a family? Does a family only consist of parents, children, and relatives? Describe your own family— does it include people who aren't related to you?

7. When Puck gets lost in the forest after his mother drowns, he has to learn to hunt in order to eat. Sabine realizes she needs to go out from "the Underneath" so she can find food for herself and Ranger, a job that Mama performed. These are just two ways that the kittens have to grow up—what are other examples?

8. Hawk Man, having turned back into a bird in order to find his daughter, spies Puck lost and hungry in the woods, and drops a mouse from the sky for Puck to eat. Name some other acts of kindness from the story.

9. As Gar Face captures Sabine in the yard, Ranger goes wild with fury and lunges at Gar Face, knocks him down, and bites him on the leg—allowing Sabine to escape. Were you surprised at Ranger's reaction? Why didn't Gar Face expect that Ranger might behave this way?

10. "You have to go back for your sister. If something happens to me, promise you'll find her" (page 77). Did you think that Puck would be able to keep this promise to his mother? Talk

about some other promises made by characters in the novel—were they kept? How, and at what cost?

11. Music plays a big role in the book, from the blues songs that Ranger bays into the moonlight to the enchanting lullabies of Night Song. Discuss music and what it means in the story. How does music help some of the characters?

12. Talk about Grandmother Moccasin. Do you think she was selfish for not telling Night Song about the rule that shape-shifters can't go back to their human form once they become an animal? Did she deserve to be imprisoned in the jar for so long? What is the lesson she learns after she's finally freed?

13. One of the novel's main themes is loss. Which of the characters have lost something, and what did they lose? Do the characters who suffer loss eventually find something new to take the place of what is gone?

14. When children don't obey to their parents in *The Underneath*, bad things happen. Who were the characters who didn't listen to their parents? What were the consequences of their disobedience? Did these characters learn from their mistakes?

15. Dogs and cats are supposed to hate each other, yet Ranger and Mama become close friends. Discuss their unlikely friendship—what were some of the things they have in common? What are other unusual friendships portrayed in the book? Do you have a friend who, on the surface, seems like someone you wouldn't ordinarily like? Why do you get along with this person?

## ACTIVITIES & PROJECTS

1. The voices of birds, animals, and reptiles tell most of the story in *The Underneath*. Write your own story from a creature's point of view, whether it's a household pet, or animal in the wild, or bird, reptile, fish, or some other living thing.

2. How does the narrative structure of *The Underneath*—where several characters take turns telling the story—resemble that of a television show? Research how to write a television screenplay. Choose one scene from the book and write a screenplay based on it, and include the characters' dialogue, the stage direction, and descriptions of the scenery.

3. Ranger the bloodhound bays mournfully about loneliness; drawn to his songs, Mama the calico cat sets out to find who sings them. Pick an emotion—loneliness, anger, fear, love—and write song lyrics, or a poem, about feelings you have.

4. The book's last chapter contains a passage about the trees of the bayou, how they could tell us what happened to Ranger, Sabine, and Puck after the story ends. Write a new last chapter for *The Underneath*, detailing what the three animals have done since they were reunited.

5. In the book, the hummingbird is described as an "intermediary" and "messenger," a being that is able to travel between life and death because it can fly so quickly. Research the mythology of some of the wild creatures in *The Underneath*—such as snakes, alligators, or hawks—and create a report about one. Illustrate your report with photographs or drawings.

Turn the page
for your first look at *Keeper*, the next novel
from Newbery Honoree Kathi Appelt.

Available May 2010
from Atheneum Books for Young Readers

"HURRY," WHISPERED KEEPER to the nighttime sky. She leaned her head back as far as she could and looked straight up. The sugary stars clung to the roof of the night and blinked back at her.

"Hurry," she said to the water beneath her tiny boat. The triangular waves brushed against its wooden sides. The dog who sat across from her whined and thumped his tail against the bottom of the boat. "B.D.," she whispered. "Best Dog." She reached toward him and rubbed the soft fur behind his ears. After a moment she let go of the dog, clasped her hands in front of her, and tucked them beneath her chin. She looked back up at the starry sky.

Where was the full moon? Shouldn't it be up by now? She was counting on the moon to pull the water back, counting on its lantern light to help her see in the dark and lead her to the sandbar only a hundred yards from the beach—especially this moon, blue moon, the second full moon of the month. Dogie had told her that a blue moon was a magic moon, good for wishing, good for praying. But so far it had not shown its creamy face.

Keeper rubbed the charm around her neck with her fingertips, let it fall against her new cotton T-shirt. The cold of it seeped through the shirt's fabric, it made a small chill, like a cold dent in her skin, where it rested right against the top of her breastbone. She took a deep breath. The dark air above the pond was thick and heavy on her shoulders, soggy.

B.D. whined, his voice a small please. *Please, can we go home now? Please?* For emphasis, he put his right front paw on her knee. *Please, please, please?* he whined.

"Best Dog," she said to him. He was worried about being in the boat this late at night when they should be sound asleep in her room next to Signe's room.

He preferred chasing dream bunnies in his sleep to chasing moonbeams in a boat. Keeper patted the paw atop her knee. She hadn't wanted to bring him along, but she needed him.

He was her "finder dog." Over the years, he had found a whole host of missing objects—the odd sock, a misplaced spoon, the tiny key to the lock on Keeper's diary, one of Signe's peace-sign earrings.

He also found other things, like one-of-a-kind seashells and tiny abandoned puppies, including Too, who was adopted by Dogie, their next-door neighbor. He found old coins and dead fish washed up on the beach. He even found shooting stars and tiny geckos, things that didn't appear to be lost.

Keeper had always relied upon him to help with finding. And tonight she needed him more than ever. As they tiptoed out the kitchen door, he hadn't made a single sound to betray her. Somehow he even managed to keep his toenails from clicking on the hard kitchen floor.

Once outside, he had loped across the grassy lawn right next to her, quiet as a marsh mouse, stepped lightly on the wooden pier so as not to make any noise, then lowered himself down into the boat with her. Having B.D. with her gave her courage, even though she could tell that he was nervous.

A small sliver of guilt rode up her wrist and settled on her tongue. She swallowed it.

Knee-to-paw, face-to-face, she looked right at him and said a true thing: "I love you, Best Dog." Then she leaned forward and wrapped her arms around him, sunk her fingers into his thick, curly fur, breathed in his doggy smell, a mixture of Purina Dog Chow and Palmolive dish soap, vestiges of his dinner and the bath she had given him earlier, added to his own peculiar B.D. smell, something like garlic and sand and honey.

She looked over his head toward the shore, where their haint blue house stood just yards away. Inside that house her empty bed waited, the cotton sheet shoved to the end of the mattress. And in the next room Signe slept, unaware that her girl and her dream bunny dog were out there. Alone. Together. In *The Scamper*. Dogie's boat.

Thinking about Signe made Keeper wince.

"We have to hurry," she told B.D. Then she patted the top of his head, and looked all around her. Looked at the three dark houses perched on the banks of this marshy pond, all cloaked in heavy shadows. She looked at the silhouettes of the sabal palms, where their resident seagull Captain slept in his nest. She saw the faint glow of the oyster shells on the road and heard the rolling breakers of the surf on the other side of the sand dunes.

"The universe unto itself," was what Signe called this place. Everyone who mattered to Keeper lived here: B.D. and Signe and Dogie and Mr. Beauchamp and Sinbad and Captain and Too. Everyone except for Meggie Marie.

For Keeper's whole entire ten-year-long life, the universe unto itself had been her home, her home with Signe and B.D. and the long-legged sandpipers and the seashells that lined her bedroom window and the shrimp boats just behind the breakers, their nets like butterfly wings dipping into the water, everything she knew and cared about, her home. But today everything had changed and now, seven years after her mother swam away on a star-filled night just like this one, Signe had said, "You don't understand, Keeper." Then she buried her face in her hands, her voice thin and narrow. "They'll take you away."

Stars, even a sky full of them, don't put out much light.

"Blue moon," Keeper said, "hurry." On the other side of the sand dunes, the rolling breakers fell, soft against the sandy beach. She looked up again at the stars. Were they the same ones that had watched her mother swim away when she was only three years old? She felt B.D. lick her knees.

"Seven years," she said to the dog. "We have to find her."

He thumped his tail against the bottom of the boat.

All those years Keeper had waited for her mother to swim back to her, had stood at the water's edge and looked out, searched the tops of waves, scanned the horizon, waited and waited and waited. But now she couldn't wait any more. Only Meggie Marie could stop the universe unto itself from coming undone. B.D. scratched a spot behind his ear with his back foot. "If she doesn't come back . . ." Keeper let the sentence trail off into the damp air.

Would her mother even recognize her? She grasped the cold charm again. She was counting on this charm, the last thing her mother had given her before she swam away.

Keeper was also counting on the carved figurines tucked beneath her bench in an old shoe box. "Gifts," she said. But they weren't for Meggie Marie, her mother. Instead, she looked out at the small dark waves of the pond and spoke, "For you, Yemaya."

"Woof," woofed B.D. His tongue washed her knee again.

She scratched the fur beneath his jaw. "We'll be back soon," she promised. "Before Signe wakes up."

At the thought of Signe, Keeper swallowed hard. Signe would never, ever, not in a million years, approve of Keeper and B.D. being out here alone in the middle of the night. And even though Signe had never told her so, Keeper knew that she did not believe in mermaids. Not in selkies or lorelei or water sprites or *meerfrau*.

*Please, please, please?* whined B.D.

Keeper's heart thumped against her rib cage in a chant: *hurry, hurry, hurry.*

Like an echo, the dog's tail thumped against the floorboards. Keeper sat back in the boat, snug against the pier, and waited for the tide to finish rising, waited for the full moon to finally pop above the horizon and turn the tide around and pull her out, pull her out to sea, take her to her mermaid mother.

"Come on, moon," she said. The charm hummed against her chest. The water rose.

"Yemaya," she whispered into the darkness. "Help us."

# NATIONAL BOOK AWARD FINALISTS

## FROM SIMON & SCHUSTER

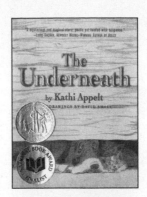

SimonandSchuster.com

# From two-time Newbery Medalist
# E. L. Konigsburg

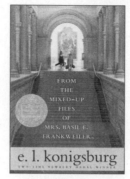

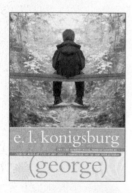

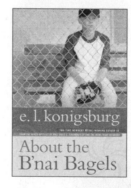

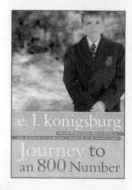

From Atheneum
Published by Simon & Schuster